RISKING THE
DREAM

Between Two Flags

An American Adventure

RISKING THE DREAM

LEE RODDY

BETHANY HOUSE PUBLISHERS
MINNEAPOLIS, MINNESOTA 55438

Published by Bethany House Publishers
A Ministry of Bethany Fellowship International
11400 Hampshire Avenue South
Bloomington, Minnesota 55438
www.bethanyhouse.com

Printed in the United States of America by
Bethany Press International, Bloomington, Minnesota 55438

Library of Congress Cataloging-in-Publication Data

Roddy, Lee, 1921-
    Risking the dream / by Lee Roddy.
        p.   cm. — (Between two flags ; 6)
Summary: As fifteen-year-old Gideon seeks work in the Confederate capital, tensions at home are inflamed by President Lincoln's ultimatum to the rebelling states.
    ISBN 0-7642-2030-6 (pbk.)
    1. Virginia—History—Civil War, 1861-1865—Juvenile fiction.
[1. Virginia—History—Civil War, 1861-1865—Fiction. 3. Slavery—Fiction.
4. Afro-Americans—Fiction. 5. Christian life—Fiction.] I. Title.
    PZ7.R6 Ri   2000
    [Fic]—dc21
                                                00-010839

To Teacher Donna Coulson
and
Librarian Kristen Puccinelli
of
St. Peter's Lutheran School,
Elk Grove, California

CONTENTS

PROLOGUE

From Gideon Tugwell's journal, December 25, 1934

I awakened long before dawn this morning and watched the silent, holy night fade while I recalled that first Christmas nearly two thousand years in the past.

I also remembered the dramatic, life-changing events that led up to this day seventy-two years ago when I was a boy. It was the second year of the Civil War. Orphaned Emily Lodge, slave Nat Travis, and I, the farm boy Gideon, were teens.

Unknown to us, each was about to be plunged into a series of suspenseful and threatening episodes. We were individually challenged with hard choices that would change us from what we were to what we would become. But the penalties for failure were terrible.

Here's how it all began. . . .

TROUBLE FOR THREE

Wednesday, October 1, 1862, Richmond, Virginia

The sound of men's angry voices drew Gideon Tugwell down the street and right into big trouble. Alone in the capital of the Confederacy for the first time in his fifteen years of life, he had a job interview scheduled with the *Richmond Sun* in a few minutes. But Gideon's curiosity prompted him to hurry around the corner to see what was happening.

A heavyset man with a red face shouted to the small group of men facing him, "That Yankee tyrant! He's got no right to say that our slaves will be free in January!"

With deeply tanned and freckled hands, Gideon drew his coat tighter against the October chill and approached the back of the crowd of men to listen. They were all older, except for a boy about Gideon's age with a thin, wedge-shaped head tapering to a sharp chin. He didn't even look at Gideon as he stopped next to him.

A gray-bearded man angrily agreed with the speaker. "That's right! Lincoln doesn't have any authority over us. We left the Union!"

The heavyset man hotly replied, "You're only half right, Henry! What if four million slaves hear about Lincoln's Emancipation Proclamation and they all rise up against us? Now that the South has just passed the second conscription act, all able-bodied men between thirty-five and forty-five are going to be fighting the Yankees alongside our younger men who're already there. That leaves only women, children, and us older . . ."

Gideon didn't catch the rest of the sentence. He released his thin coat and reached into his pocket to produce a stub of pencil and a piece of paper. He began rapidly scribbling, unmindful of the biting wind ruffling his straw-colored hair. His mother had cut it for him just before he left their small farm near Church Creek in Virginia's inland Piedmont area.

The boy standing next to him whispered in a heavy Southern accent, "What're you doing?"

"Oh, nothing much," Gideon whispered back. He was reluctant to say that someday he planned to be a writer, so he jotted down things that he might use in a story.

The boy demanded, "You a Yankee spy?"

"Of course not!" Gideon's blue eyes focused on hazel ones.

"Then why're you writing down what they're saying?"

Aware that the men were turning toward him, Gideon decided it was not worthwhile explaining his purpose. "I'm going to be late for an appointment," he said and hurried back around the corner. As he reached it, he turned and glanced back. Now everyone in the group was looking at him. The boy started following him. Gideon couldn't risk being late for his appointment after traveling so far. He broke into a run.

★ ★ ★ ★ ★

Emily Lodge's soft carpet slippers made no sound as she walked down Briarstone's long hallway toward her cousin William's library. She suppressed a sigh, knowing that almost anything she said to him could result in another of their frequent disagreements.

She paused outside the partially open door upon hearing a young feminine voice say as if to herself, "Dat's a *b*, an' dat's a *c*."

Emily peered cautiously around the door to see Molly, a slave girl of about ten, holding a feather duster in her right hand. Her left hand gently rested on the pages of an open book.

Fascinated by the intent look on the maid's face, Emily didn't hear anyone come up behind her.

"What're you doing?" William asked.

Emily whirled around to see him with his ever-present body

★ ★

servant, Levi, behind him. "Oh!" Emily exclaimed. "You startled me!" Behind her she heard the maid slam the book closed.

William Lodge was seventeen, strongly built, with a mind of his own. He had been Briarstone's acting master since his father formed a cavalry unit and rode off to fight the invading Union armies. "Well?" he prompted. Emily, a very pretty girl with fair skin, long blond hair, and small features, explained, "I was looking for you—"

"What's that sound?" he interrupted, stepping closer and shoving the door open with well-muscled arms. He raised his voice. "Molly! You know better than to touch the pages of a book! Only dust the covers."

She didn't meet his eyes but hastily declared, "Yessa, Massa."

"You can finish that later," he told her and stood aside to let her scurry past him. Emily caught a terrified look on Molly's face and guessed that she knew Emily had seen her trying to read.

Emily followed William into the cozy, dark-paneled room filled with the fragrance of fine leather. Levi silently trailed them with downcast eyes.

William motioned for Emily to take one of two matching wing chairs placed below each of two windows that bordered the small fireplace. She sat, her violet eyes sweeping the remaining three walls. They were covered with glass-fronted bookcases that protected hundreds of leather-bound volumes.

William started to seat himself in the chair that had been his father's favorite but abruptly stopped. "I left this book open," he mused. "Molly knows she's only supposed to dust and not touch— oh!" He glanced accusingly at Emily. "She's been looking at it, and that's your fault!"

"Mine?"

"Yes! I'm sure she's been listening to you teach the overseer's brats, and you know it's against the law for a slave to learn to read or write!"

"I haven't taught anyone except the Toombs family!"

"Don't tell me that! I've told you before: I don't want my pickaninnies educated!"

"Why not? If President Lincoln's Emancipation Proclamation

frees four million slaves, how're they going to make a living with no skills and no education?"

"That tyrant can never enforce such a plan as long as the Confederacy stands! I'm not going to tell you again—stop interfering with my servants! Now, why did you want to see me?"

Emily knew he was in no mood to grant her request. She replied, "It doesn't matter," and hurried away before she again spoke her mind and created more trouble.

★　★　★　★　★

Nat, William's sixteen-year-old former body slave, was on his way to the south drawing room when he saw Emily rush away from the young master's library. Nat frowned, sensing that something was wrong. He entered the room with a basket of kindling for the fireplace.

He smiled at an attractive new fifteen-year-old maid who was polishing the twin candlesticks on the wooden mantel. "Morning, Delia," he said with a smile while lowering the basket in front of the fireplace. "How come you're working downstairs today?"

Like Nat, she had dark eyes and hair, light brown skin, and Caucasian facial features, indicating they had white fathers. At five ten, Nat was a good six inches taller than Delia. She didn't return his smile but glanced around and lowered her voice.

"The young mistresses are talking privately and sent me away. Besides, I had to speak to you, so when I saw you go for the wood, I came here. I heard something you should know."

She was one of the few Briarstone slaves besides Nat who spoke proper English instead of the dialect. But there was something in her tone that concerned him. "What's that?"

"You remember that Levi became the young master's body servant when he sent you to the fields?"

It was such an obvious question that Nat merely nodded. He had only recently been restored to the big house after helping stop a slave uprising. However, William had not given him his old job back.

Delia placed a candlestick on the mantel and lowered her voice.

★　★

"Now Levi is afraid the master will send him to the fields and make you his body servant again."

Nat shrugged. The big house was always full of rumors and intrigue. "I'm not concerned. I like the freedom of working all over this house instead of following William like a dog."

"Just the same," Delia warned, "please be careful."

"I will." His smile returned. "You going to go hear Brother Tynes Sunday night?"

"Shh!" Delia's brown eyes flickered around the room. Slave preachers were prohibited by law, so secret church services were held deep in the woods where the master could not hear the singing and shouting. She added, "I'll be there. Will you?"

"If I can get away. But I could never do that when I was William's personal servant."

Delia gave him a fleeting smile as she walked out. "I'll look for you there. Meanwhile, watch out for Levi."

Nat would miss her if he succeeded in his next planned escape. He hoped to find Amos, one of his younger brothers. Nat had heard Amos was a slave on a small nearby plantation. The brothers hadn't seen each other since their first master died and heirs split the family by selling each one to separate masters eighteen months ago. Nat hoped they could escape together on the secret Underground Railroad. But freedom was a lofty goal, so Nat put the thought aside and frowned as he recalled Delia's warning. More concerned about Levi than he cared to admit, Nat started laying the firewood for later that night.

★　★　★　★　★

Emily jumped up on her cousin Julie's high four-poster bed and shook her head. "Your brother and I just clashed again," Emily declared.

Dark-haired Julie, who was fourteen, looked up from where she was examining a dress hanging in her armoire. "Oh? What about this time?"

Emily liked Julie, who was the exact opposite of outspoken, strong-minded Emily. Julie was a soft-spoken Southern girl, well-mannered and submissive, especially around her domineering older brother.

Emily briefly explained about William's accusation. "Sometimes," Emily finished with a gentle sigh, "I wonder why my family all died and I had to come as an orphan to live here. Oh," she added hastily, "you and I are good friends, but your brother makes it clear that he wishes I were someplace else."

Julie critically examined the dress, which opened up the front instead of down the back, as most garments did for girls her age. "Do you think I should wear this to church Sunday?"

"It looks good to me," Emily answered absently. "I keep telling myself that I believe God keeps me here in the Confederacy for a reason, but I'd still love to return home to Illinois. It would be especially wonderful to spend Christmas with Jessie."

Jessie Barlow and Emily had been best friends for years. She and her mother had extended a standing invitation for Emily to come stay with them anytime.

"Christmas," Julie mused, holding the dress against her in front of the dresser mirror. "Do you think Gideon will be back here before then?"

"Not if he gets that job in Richmond, which I hope he does because he wants it so much." She silently added, *But if that happens, will I ever see him again?*

Both girls turned toward the closed door at the sound of a gentle knock.

When Julie called, "Come in," Delia entered.

"Excuse me, Miss Emily, but Master William wants to see you right away."

"Thank you, Delia. Did he say what he wanted?"

"No, Miss Emily, but he was not happy."

"Now what?" Emily asked and slid off the high bed.

★　★　★　★　★

Gideon was a little out of breath when he pushed through the *Sun*'s front door. He hoped the editor wouldn't sense how desperately he needed the job. Gideon didn't want to return home a fail-

★　★

TROUBLE FOR THREE

ure. Emily had told him that's what William expected because Gideon was "poor white trash."

The good smell of newsprint and the rhythmic sound of presses greeted him as he approached the bespectacled little man behind the counter. Trying to speak calmly, Gideon introduced himself, adding, "I have an appointment with the editor, Mr. Buford Kerr."

The clerk glanced at a sheet of paper on the counter. "You're last on his list. I'll tell him you're here."

"Thank you." Gideon tried to calm his anxiety as the man pushed through a swinging door. Gideon had traveled three days to apply for an errand boy's job. He hoped that being around a daily newspaper would help him become a better writer and that someday he would be an author and write books.

He turned when the front door opened and the thin-faced boy who'd challenged him moments before walked in.

"So," he said to Gideon, "this is where you disappeared to so fast."

"I have an appointment here," Gideon explained.

"Me too. I'm going to be their new errand boy."

Gideon blinked in surprise. He had expected that there would be other candidates for the job, but he had a bad feeling about competing with this boy.

The clerk returned and told Gideon, "Mr. Kerr will see you now. This way, please."

As Gideon started to follow the man, the other boy whispered, "You're wasting your time! That job is mine!"

Gideon knew he shouldn't let it bother him, but it added to his secret fear that he wasn't really good enough to work at a newspaper. He tried to shake off his doubts as he entered the editor's glass-enclosed office for the most important meeting in his young life.

★ ★

17

HOPE OUT OF DISASTER

Gideon timidly entered the office where Buford Kerr sat at a rolltop desk overflowing with untidy papers. Gideon wasn't sure what an editor looked like, but this one was in his fifties, short and stocky, with wild gray hair and matching untrimmed beard. Red braces held up baggy gray pants.

"Sit!" he ordered without looking up from where he was slashing viciously at a sheet of paper with a pencil.

"Yes, sir," Gideon replied, his uneasiness growing as he gingerly eased into a rickety straight-back chair.

"Blasted war!" Kerr exclaimed, taking a final slash at the paper. He tossed it into a small box marked *Out* and turned bloodshot eyes on Gideon. "All the good reporters have been conscripted to fight in the army, and those who're left can't write their own names. Now all I have to choose from is boys. You want to be a reporter?"

Gideon gulped before replying, "Yes, sir, someday. I hope to start work here as an errand boy."

"You brought something for me to read?" Kerr's tone was sharp and quick. "Samples of your writing?"

"Uh . . . no, I didn't think—"

"Didn't think!" the editor interrupted curtly. "How can I put out a newspaper with unthinking incompetents?"

Gideon felt foolish for not having thought of bringing some of his work, but he was really hurt by the man's rough manner. "I'm willing to learn, sir," he said a little lamely. "I'll try hard—"

"I've heard that before," Kerr broke in. "Thanks for coming."

★   ★

He stood, indicating the interview was over.

Gideon blinked, stunned and crushed that he had traveled so far to be rejected so quickly. "Sir, if you'll just give me a chance—" he began but again was interrupted.

"On your way out, tell my clerk to send in that boy who was here before. Name's Hassler, I think he said."

Devastated emotionally, Gideon reentered the front office and repeated Kerr's instructions to the clerk. The boy he'd seen before jumped up with a triumphant grin.

"Max Hassler, that's me!" He lowered his voice as he passed Gideon, saying, "I told you that job was mine!"

★   ★   ★   ★   ★

Emily knocked at the closed library door, then entered at William's call to come in. She asked, "You wanted to see me?"

"Yes, and you also wanted to ask about something a while ago. First, have you seen my account book?"

"No. I don't even know what it looks like."

"It's about so big." William indicated a medium-sized book with his hands. "It's where I keep all my financial records. I've asked all the servants, and even my mother and sister, but they haven't seen it, either. I hoped maybe you had."

"Sorry. I'll help you look if you want."

"No, that's all right. But it's strange because that's the second thing that's recently disappeared from this library. A ten-dollar gold piece my grandfather gave me years ago is also missing."

"Could you have mislaid it?"

"No, I didn't mislay either the book or the coin." William's tone hardened. "Maybe that little black imp Molly took it. Anyway, what was it you wanted to see me about a while ago?"

"I wondered if you'd mind if I took a carriage instead of riding horseback to visit Gideon's mother."

"Don't bother me with questions like that, Emily! Do whichever you want, but don't take anything where you'll need a driver. I want old George on hand at all times."

"Thanks, William." Emily again turned to leave, but his voice stopped her.

★   ★

"Why do you want to see that Tugwell woman?"

Flinching at the disapproving tone, Emily explained, "I like her, that's why."

"You mean you really want to find out if she's heard if her white trash son reached Richmond safely."

"Please don't refer to Gideon that way!"

"He won't get the job, Emily. Face it! He's nothing but a dirt farmer's son, and all his talk about being an author is hogwash! He'll come crawling back like a whipped dog because he's never going to amount to anything!"

Emily bit her tongue to keep back an angry retort. "I think you're wrong, William," she said with forced quietness. "You'll see!"

She stepped through the door and closed it quickly before he could reply. Hurrying down the long hallway, she silently fumed, *Why can't he and I ever have a conversation without it getting uncomfortable? I think he really wishes I'd go back to Illinois. Well, so do I! But I can't get passes through the Confederate and Union lines because of the war!*

★　★　★　★　★

Gideon didn't answer Max Hassler's taunting words but rushed out the front door as a sudden mist flooded his eyes. He hadn't been so miserable since his father suddenly collapsed and died of heart failure.

"Watch it!" a man's voice broke through his misery.

"Sorry!" Gideon mumbled, glancing at the bearded man just entering the door. Gideon stepped to one side just as the stranger did the same, again bringing them face-to-face. He had a full brown beard and wore a butternut-colored Confederate uniform.

"Whoa!" the man said with a friendly grin. "You stand still and I'll walk around you. Otherwise, we might be here all week."

Too numb with disappointment to even answer, Gideon stopped, keeping his face down so his eyes couldn't be seen. The man started to go past him, then hesitated. "Uh . . . something wrong?"

Gideon shook his head. At fifteen, he told himself he was too

★　★

old to cry, and especially in front of a stranger. He started to leave but felt a hand gently touch his forearm.

"Look, it's none of my business, but I have a hunch the same thing happened to you just now that happened to me nearly twenty years ago. You just lose a job here?"

"I applied but didn't get it."

"I know how you feel," the stranger said, jerking his chin toward the editor's office. "That curmudgeon did the same thing to me when I first applied here." Pausing, the man smiled knowingly at Gideon before saying, "My name's Herb Hunter. I worked here until the South's conscription act forced those of us between thirty-five and forty-five to join the military. Say, I haven't had breakfast. Have you?"

Gideon hadn't but didn't want to admit that. His only money was a carefully hoarded prewar U.S. minted twenty-dollar gold piece. His mother had given it to him, but he considered it a loan to be repaid. Since his trip had been in vain, he didn't want to spend any more than was necessary. He said, "I can't, thanks anyway."

"It's on me," the man said casually. "And call me Herb. I came to visit with Kerr and complain about being in the military, but that can wait. So will you join me?"

Gideon hesitated, looking at Herb Hunter's warm blue eyes and friendly grin. Gideon was about an inch taller than the man.

Impulsively, Gideon spoke. "All right, but I can't stay long. I have to call on a widow woman I met once before."

★   ★   ★   ★   ★

Nat was surprised when William ordered him to go tell George to have the town coach ready in the morning. As Nat approached the carriage house, he recalled that Levi had frowned when the young master sent Nat to do what usually would have been Levi's assignment. But Nat forgot that when he found Delia talking to George, the old carriage driver. George was also Nat's only close friend.

Nat saw the gray-haired reinsman holding up his bright green livery, with the gold buttons on his swallow-tailed coat and matching pants, while Delia examined it.

She smiled warmly at Nat, who returned the smile. She was certainly pretty, he silently admitted.

George greeted Nat by saying, "I'm surprised the young master let you out of the big house." George did not speak in slave dialect, having taught himself to use proper English from years of listening to the masters while driving them various places.

"So'm I," Delia said. "The mistress sent me to be sure George had replaced a button he recently lost from his jacket."

She was the only slave on Briarstone Plantation who knew that Nat and George could speak without dialect. In front of others, they used the common slave tongue.

Nat shifted his eyes to George. "William sent me to tell you he wants the town carriage ready tomorrow morning."

George's eyebrows arched. "Oh? I would have expected him to send Levi instead of you."

Nat glanced at Delia and guessed from her serious expression that she was thinking about the warning she had given him earlier. "I don't know why he sent me," Nat admitted. He stole another glance at Delia and added reluctantly, "Well, I'd better go back inside."

George surprised him by saying, "Before you go, what rumors are going on in the big house about Lincoln freeing all the slaves at the first of the year?"

The old driver had never expressed interest in what was going on in the manor house. His question suggested Delia might have said something to him about this.

"I don't listen to what the others say," Nat said evasively. Delia was new to Briarstone, and when Nat first came here, George had warned him to never trust anyone, including the other slaves. Some would betray a confidence to the master for a small trinket.

"But you must have some idea of what will happen," Delia prompted.

Cautiously, Nat shook his head. "I've heard that the owners say they don't expect anything to happen unless the North wins the war. They don't think that's likely."

★ ★

"But if the Union does win," Delia persisted, "what do you think will happen to all of us?"

On his guard, Nat hesitated before answering. He could hardly wait to be free, having twice run away and been recaptured. His next try would be even more risky because of trying to find his brother Amos so they could flee to freedom together. Nat replied to Delia's question with his own. "What do *you* think will happen?"

"I don't know."

George said, "Well, I know what I'd like to do. I want to live out the rest of my days on this place. I was born here somewhere around sixty-three years ago, and I wouldn't want to be anyplace else."

Nat wanted to stay and get to know Delia better, but it wasn't wise to linger on a small errand. He again smiled at her and left.

★　★　★　★　★

While they studied the menu at a small restaurant, Hunter asked where Gideon was from and why he wanted a newspaper job.

Gideon was reluctant to tell this uniformed stranger about his personal problems, but Herb Hunter seemed to genuinely care. Gideon took a deep breath and began.

"I live on a small farm near Church Creek with my mother, a younger brother, and two sisters. Our father's dead." Gideon paused when Herb said he was sorry, then told of his heart's desire to become an author, and his belief that working on a newspaper would improve his writing skills. He mentioned meeting the thin-faced boy on the street and Buford Kerr's curt interview.

Gideon concluded, "I want that job so much! I'm sure I'd do it well, and I don't want to go home a failure."

Herb laid his menu on the table. "Do you know anyone in Richmond besides the widow you mentioned?"

"No. Well, I met a girl named Hannah who lives with Mrs. Stonum. She wrote a friend of mine in Church Creek that she knows a woman here who boards and rooms boys. I have to tell Mrs. Stonum I won't need a place to live."

"Aren't you going to try getting on at any of the other news-

★　★
24

papers like the *Examiner, Whig, Enquirer, Dispatch*, or *Southern Illustrated News*?

"I'd like to, but I have only twenty dollars to my name. If I spend that and still don't get a job, I'd not only have to go home in shame, but I'd have spent the money, and our family can't afford that."

Gideon bit his tongue. *I'm talking too much!*

"Say!" Hunter exclaimed, "I have an idea about how you might still work your way into a newspaper job."

Gideon's hopes flared up. "You do?"

"Yes, so let's order, then I'll tell you what I have in mind. Later, I'll give you a ride to the widow's."

Gideon remembered his mother's admonition about being wary of strangers in the big city. Some of them would try to steal his money, and he had already told Hunter about his double eagle.

"Look, Gideon," Hunter said, seeming to sense the boy's uncertainty. "I hit this town when I was maybe a year or two older than you, and I got the same kick in the teeth you just did. But a kind man gave me a hand, and frankly, I'd feel as if I were paying him back if I could do the same for someone else—someone like you."

Gideon decided to take a chance. "All right, tell me your idea."

★   ★   ★   ★   ★

After reporting to William that he had relayed his message to George, Nat silently started up the stairs to trim all the lamp wicks in the bedchambers. A sound under the stairwell made him abruptly stop. Nat usually slept there on a corn-shuck pallet. He glanced down and saw Levi hurriedly walk away from the area under the stairs.

What was Levi doing in my area? Nat wondered. He thought about going down to ask but decided against it. *He couldn't be stealing because I don't own a single thing.* Shrugging, Nat continued up the stairs.

DECISIONS AND DOUBTS

Emily and Julie had a buggy brought around for them to visit Gideon's mother. As Emily drove the horse along the dirt road, Julie shook her dark hair.

"I can't understand why you're so set on going to see her. There's no way she could have yet heard anything from Gideon. His appointment isn't until today."

"I didn't expect to know if he got the job. But he might have sent a wire saying he arrived safely."

"I don't think so. That costs too much money, and the military keeps the line tied up most of the time."

Emily mused, "I can't get over how surprised I was that your brother not only provided transportation for Gideon to Richmond but even gave him some pocket money. I mean, considering how much William dislikes Gideon."

Julie exclaimed, "I'm usually the naïve one, but this time it's you! William wanted Gideon away from here for a while, so he helped him go apply for that job."

Emily turned violet eyes to her cousin's hazel ones. "Why does William want Gideon away from here?"

"You'd know if you thought about it. What does William want from the Tugwells more than anything else?"

Emily replied, "Why, to buy their land, of course. But Gideon's father wouldn't sell when he was alive, and Gideon's mother and older brother won't sell now."

"My brother would do almost anything to get that prime piece of bottomland. He thinks that would greatly increase our father's respect if William got that land."

Emily protested, "I know how much he wants to force the Tugwells off their land, but you're just guessing about what William would do to get it."

"No, I'm not!" Julie exclaimed. "Fact is, I heard him tell Barley Cobb to frighten that freed slave who is working for the Tugwells so that he will quit."

"Dilly?" Emily frowned, not understanding. "Why would William and Cobb bother him? He's just helping out at the Tugwells' until Gideon comes home."

"What if he gets the job and stays in Richmond?"

Emily's eyes slowly opened wide in understanding. "If Dilly didn't stay, the Tugwells' hired man couldn't handle the place by himself; not with having only one hand. They'd have to sell their farm, which is the only way they can make a living!"

"Exactly! My brother is young, but he's smart!"

"I can't let him do that!" Emily cried. "I'll talk to him—"

"No!" Julie interrupted. "If you say anything to him, he'll know I told you and I'll be in big trouble!"

Emily didn't want that to happen. She tried to think how to thwart William's plan. Whatever she did, she knew he would be furious. He might order her to leave as he had done once before. If it happened again, he wouldn't let her return.

★　★　★　★　★

After breakfast, Gideon and Hunter entered a hack and gave the driver instructions to Mrs. Stonum's home. Gideon was excited about the correspondent's idea of how he might still get a job at the *Sun*, but Gideon didn't forget his manners. "Thanks for breakfast, Mr. Hunter."

"You're welcome. I go there a lot. The owner is from Missouri, and he still serves a country-style breakfast. I like his hot corn pone, hot biscuits, buttermilk, and what passes as coffee these days. As you know, the Union blockade has cut off many supplies, especially coffee."

"I liked the buttermilk." Gideon quickly came back to his

★　★

host's idea. "Let's see if I understand what you have in mind for me to do. You resent the military system that tries to keep the public from what you feel readers have a right to know. You think you can persuade Mr. Kerr to pay me to deliver some stories you'll write about what's really going on inside your military camp. Right?"

"Right, except nobody outside the newspaper office is to know I'm the one filing the stories. I might be court-martialed if my superior officers found out."

Gideon shifted uneasily in the seat. "I don't want to do anything illegal."

"I figured as much. All you'll be doing is acting as a private courier, for which you'll get paid. Of course, as I said, whatever stories you write for the paper, I'll look at and help polish. If you're really that good of a writer, Kerr will someday give you a chance as a correspondent."

Gideon fell silent as the hack's horse clopped along the street. This was an opportunity that Gideon had not expected. It sounded wonderful, but William's mocking voice intruded into the happy thought. *"You're nothing but poor white trash and will never be anything more than just a dirt farmer."*

Maybe he's right, Gideon reluctantly admitted. *If so, why should I pursue an impossible dream of being a writer when my family has such great needs?*

Shaking his head, Gideon asked himself, *But is it better to stay and take a chance that I might make it instead of going home? There I know William will sneer and tell Emily, "I told you so!" But my mother and John Fletcher need me to help on the farm. Isn't that more important than what William says?*

Unable to decide, Gideon said, "I have a problem, Mr. Hunter. I really want to work for the paper. But since I didn't get the job I came here for, if I stay to work for you, then I'm putting my personal ambition above my family's need for my help on the farm. I'm not sure what would be the right thing for me to do."

"I understand your problem," Hunter replied. "But it has to be your decision. You think about it while we visit with your friend Mrs. Stonum."

★ ★

★ ★ ★ ★ ★

As Nat trimmed the blackened wicks of each coal oil lamp in every bedchamber, he became curious about why Levi had been around his sleeping quarters. Nat ended his chores and returned to the area under the stairs.

He stood looking thoughtfully at his corn-shuck mattress and a pair of William's cast-off shoes he had handed down to his former body slave. There was nothing to indicate either had been touched. Nat looked up and smiled as Delia came down the hallway.

She smiled back, teasingly asking, "You thinking of going to bed in the daytime?"

He chuckled. No household slave slept until all the white folks were in bed. Maids and other household help slept in whatever places they could: outside the masters' or mistresses' doors, in the stair landings, and wherever they would be instantly at hand if called.

Nat kept his voice down so that no one else could hear and answered Delia's question. "I saw Levi leaving here a while ago. I'm trying to find out what he's up to."

Delia said, "Remember what I told you. Don't trust him."

Grinning, Nat admitted, "I've got nothing to steal unless he wants some old dried-up corn shucks."

"Just the same," Delia answered. "Remember that I warned you about him." She hurried down the long hallway.

Nat forgot about Levi as he watched Delia moving away. *Stop it!* he reprimanded himself. *Slaves have no rights at all, not even to think about the future or someone they'd like to know better.*

Nat jumped. *But if I escape to freedom, someday maybe . . .* He returned to thinking how he might run away on his third try for freedom.

★ ★ ★ ★ ★

With Hunter beside him, Gideon pulled the doorbell at Lydia Stonum's two-story frame house. Gideon tried to settle his thoughts about whether to accept Herb Hunter's offer or promptly return to help on his family's farm.

★ ★

An attractive girl with shoulder-length brunette hair opened the door and peered out.

"Hannah?" Gideon asked uncertainly.

"Yes. Do I know you? Oh! Gideon!" She gave a glad cry and whirled around to call back into the room. "Mrs. Stonum! It's Gideon Tugwell!"

Gideon's gaze took in her high-necked blouse with long sleeves and buttons down the front. He repeated something often said to him. "You've grown! I hardly recognized you."

"I'm thirteen now." She turned to look at the man.

Gideon introduced them. "Hannah Chandler, this is Herb Hunter. He was a correspondent for the *Sun* until recently."

"Now you're a soldier," Hannah said approvingly. "My father was until he got killed fighting the Yankees. My mother died of fever. Come in! Give me your coats!"

As they did, Gideon told Hunter, "She works in a munitions factory, making percussion caps and loading cartridges with gunpowder."

Hunter whistled. "That must be highly dangerous!"

"It can be," Hannah admitted. "Some girls are as young as nine. But we're all doing our part to help our boys win this terrible war."

"There's a story you could write," the correspondent told Gideon as Mrs. Stonum, a slender forty-three-year-old widow, hurried down from upstairs. She had parted her brown hair in the middle and pulled it back in the current style.

"Gideon, welcome!" she exclaimed, crossing to take both his hands. "How did the job interview go?"

Before replying, Gideon introduced Hunter and then all were seated in the front parlor. Gideon recounted his unhappy job interview, concluding, "So I came by to thank you for arranging a place for me to stay with your friend Mrs. Crockett, but I may not need it."

At the disappointed look on both Mrs. Stonum's and Hannah's faces, Gideon promptly added, "But I'm thinking of an offer Mr. Hunter made me if I stay here awhile."

The widow turned to the correspondent, who quickly

recounted the proposition he had extended to Gideon.

"Take it, Gideon!" Hannah cried when Herb finished. Instantly, she dropped her eyes and a faint tinge of color touched her cheeks.

Gideon was surprised and a little abashed.

Mrs. Stonum smoothly asked, "What about everyone at Church Creek, Gideon? Your family, Emily, and the others? Are they all well?"

"Fine, thanks." Gideon summarized how each was doing, ending with Emily.

"I miss her," Hannah said. "She and I shared a bedchamber while she was here for some months. Has she given up on ever getting back home to Illinois?"

"No, not really, but she told me that she has accepted the fact that apparently God wants her to be here in the South, at least for a while."

Mrs. Stonum asked, "Do you think she really would still go home if she could get the passes?"

"I'm sure of it," Gideon assured her. "But after you went to all that trouble to get passes through the lines, and then you both got turned back at the Battle of Second Manassas, well, she just accepted it."

Hannah exclaimed, "Mrs. Stonum, Emily has already qualified for passes, and you personally know General Robert E. Lee and President Jefferson Davis. Why don't you ask one of them to give Emily new passes?"

The widow replied. "I'll think about that." Turning to Hunter, she asked, "What do you do in our military?"

He grinned. "I keep trying to get out, but our Jeff Davis's conscription act keeps me in this uniform when I would rather be back writing for the *Sun*."

"You have a family?" Hannah asked him.

"No. Never been married. But I made a little money outside the newspaper, so I am content except for the frustration the military places on me as a reporter."

Hannah said, "Gideon, you've always wanted to be a writer! Just because you didn't get the errand boy's job doesn't mean you have to go home. Why not take Mr. Hunter up on his offer?"

★ ★

Gideon hadn't resolved his mental conflict about whether it would be right for him to do that instead of returning to the farm. "Well . . ." he said uncertainly.

Mrs. Stonum surprised Gideon by suggesting, "As long as you're here, why not at least give it a try? Maybe for a couple weeks—that is, if Mr. Hunter agrees?"

"Sure!" the correspondent exclaimed heartily. "It would give me a chance to get the stories out that I want to see printed, and Gideon could see if he likes it well enough to stay on. Otherwise, he could go home with his head up, knowing he had done what he came for."

"Then do it!" Hannah exclaimed. "I'll tell you how to get to where Mrs. Crockett lives. Then you can have a place to stay and something to eat while you're here!"

Gideon, rattled by the sudden turn of events, stammered, "Well, I . . . I—"

Mrs. Stonum broke in, "Of course, you're welcome to visit here, too, Gideon. In fact, why don't you and Mr. Hunter return for supper tonight? Not only can we catch up on everything that way, but I'd like to tell you about a young drummer boy at Chimborazo Hospital, where I'm a volunteer nurse. I think you could write his story and get it published. His name's Zebulon Trotter."

"Zeb Trotter?" Gideon cried in disbelief. "A boy younger than I? A drummer?"

"Yes!" Mrs. Stonum exclaimed. "You know him?"

"We had some exciting adventures at the First Battle of Manassas," Gideon replied. "He's wounded?"

"Yes, at Antietam in Maryland. They found him unconscious and wounded in the arm. Like many of our boys wounded in that battle, he was barefooted. He's recovering from his wound, but emotionally . . ."

She didn't finish the thought but added quickly, "It's not uncommon, even among older soldiers. But he must have seen some horrible things while going into battles carrying nothing but a drum!"

Concerned, Gideon said, "I'd like to see him."

"Good!" Hannah exclaimed. "Then it's settled!"

★ ★

Gideon hadn't meant that as a commitment, because he was still concerned about his family. However, before he could clarify himself, the widow spoke again.

"Mr. Hunter, forgive us for being so excited. But is all of this agreeable with you?"

"Absolutely! I'd also like to hear some of your stories about working with wounded soldiers." Hunter turned to Gideon. "What do you say?"

Numbly, Gideon nodded, then instantly felt his heart lurch. A small, annoying voice seemed to silently chide him. *Are you sure you're not going to regret this?*

★ ★ ★ ★ ★

In visiting Gideon's mother in her small kitchen, Emily debated whether to mention what Julie had said about her brother's and Barley Cobb's plan to frighten off the Tugwells' freedman. It was a difficult decision for Emily because the small widow's face already showed long, furrowed lines gouged by a lifetime of barely scratching out a living on a hardscrabble farm.

Sipping buttermilk because tea and coffee were so scarce, Martha Tugwell confessed, "I have mixed feelings about Gideon in Richmond. I want him to get that job because he wants so much to be a writer, yet my mother's heart aches to have him home."

She sighed softly before adding, "I try to be grateful to our Lord for John Fletcher and Dilly helping out while Gideon's away. But it's hard sometimes, being a widow with a stepson away fighting the invaders, and my little girls and their brother Ben being too young to help much with all the chores."

Emily glanced at Julie before saying, "I'm sure it is. Speaking of Dilly, how's he working out?"

"Oh, he's wonderful! He and Mr. Fletcher get along so well, and—" She interrupted herself as the family's two hounds suddenly bawled and ran down the long, rutted lane baying at someone.

Mrs. Tugwell peered out the window and exclaimed in dismay,

★ ★

"Oh no! It's that awful Barley Cobb!"

"The slave catcher?" Emily asked.

"Yes," Gideon's mother cried. "I hope he's not going to propose marriage to me again!"

THREATS AND THIEVERY

Emily turned from Julie to watch Gideon's mother as she opened the door a crack. She ordered the hounds to be quiet, then looked up at Barley Cobb without inviting him in. He was a rough-looking man in his middle forties, wearing military-style boots extending almost to his knees.

"Howdy, Martha," he said through an untrimmed and tobacco-stained brown beard. He swept off a battered slouch hat, which allowed uncombed, shoulder-length hair to spill down in back and on both sides of his head. His small eyes shifted from the widow to the girls.

Emily took a step backward as he grinned at her, showing crooked teeth stained with the chewing tobacco wad that made an unsightly lump in his left cheek.

"Reckon yore William's kin, ain't you?" he asked.

Mrs. Tugwell spoke coolly before Emily could. "Mr. Cobb, I'm a Christian woman, so I don't like to say what I have to right now. But I've told you before that I don't want you to call here."

He didn't seem to be the least concerned about her firm words. "I done fergive ye a'fore fer having a widder woman's bitter tongue. But seein' as how I'm a-gonna marry up with ye someday, it'd be the neighborly thing to ask to sit a spell and offer me a glass o' buttermilk a'fore I ride on."

Emily felt sorry for Mrs. Tugwell as she hesitated. Emily recalled Gideon telling her of the twice-married but childless widower who vainly tried wooing Gideon's mother since her husband died more than a year ago.

Martha Tugwell shook her graying hair. "Mr. Cobb, I have given you my final word on marriage, and I don't like you coming around, especially when my son is away."

Still showing no sign of affront, Cobb replied, "If he stays on in Richmond, ye'll be a-needin' some he'p around this here place. Seeing as how ye only got that one-handed man and a black boy to do the work, ye'll be needin' a real man to he'p ye. So if I was you—"

"Mr. Cobb!" Mrs. Tugwell interrupted with a flash of annoyance. "I'm about to close this door! I don't want it to hurt you when I do!"

Emily sucked in her breath as anger finally showed in Cobb's little pig eyes. "Reckon I know when I ain't welcome," he replied curtly. "Only don't ye come crawlin' to me when yore farm gits sold out from under yore nose!"

★ ★ ★ ★ ★

When Gideon and Hunter returned to Mrs. Stonum's for supper, the boy was almost glowing with happiness. He told how Hunter had taken him back to the *Sun*, where the editor agreed to give Gideon a two-weeks' paid trial as a courier. Feeling elated in spite of the glare Max Hassler directed at him as they left, Gideon accepted Hunter's hack ride to meet Mrs. Beulah Crockett. She agreed to let him board there and share a room with another boy who was temporarily away visiting relatives.

When Gideon finished excitedly recounting those events, Hannah smiled across the dinner table at him. She said, "I'm so glad for you, Gideon! I hope we can be friends like Emily and I were while she was here."

A little uncertain about her unexpectedly direct remark, Gideon only nodded.

Mrs. Stonum passed a plate of boiled potatoes to him, saying, "So now you're really working for a newspaper. I'm happy for you, too, Gideon."

"Thanks," he said, forking a potato onto his plate.

Hannah asked, "But isn't that going to be dangerous, Gideon? Those mean Yankees could be anywhere between Mr. Hunter's army camp outside of Fredericksburg and Richmond. Not to mention the lawless gangs now roaming the streets to rob and beat decent people."

Gideon had been so thrilled about his good fortune that he hadn't considered any hazards. He glanced at the correspondent. "Is it dangerous, Mr. Hunter?"

The newspaper man pursed his lips thoughtfully before answering. "Well, in wartime, there's always some element of risk, but if you stay away from the fighting, you should be safe enough."

Gideon felt a tingle of alarm. "But the fighting moves around real fast sometimes, doesn't it?"

"Sometimes," Hunter admitted. "But I've seen enough of you to believe you can take care of yourself."

Mrs. Stonum tried to sound confident. "Being a courier between Mr. Hunter's camp and Richmond certainly cannot be as dangerous as what your friend Zebulon encounters marching into battle carrying nothing but a drum."

True, Gideon thought, feeling more concern that his new job might not be as safe as he wished. To change the subject, Gideon said, "Mrs. Stonum, I'd like to see Zeb and write his story. Maybe the *Sun* will publish it. When do you think I could visit him?"

"I'll check with the surgeon tomorrow," she replied. "Now, tell me more about Emily. How is she holding up under the repeated frustrations about getting home to Illinois?"

Gideon put down his fork and answered thoughtfully. "Other than what I told you before, I can't think of anything except that her cousin William makes life difficult for her to live at Briarstone. So it's easy to understand why Emily wants to go back home and live with her best friend, Jessie Barlow."

Hannah exclaimed, "Oh, Mrs. Stonum, you said you'd think about asking General Lee or President Davis about passes for Emily. When can you make that decision?"

"I've already made it," the widow replied.

At the joyous expression on Gideon's face, she hastily added, "But when the army gave passes for Emily and me as her chaperon, we had to turn back because of a battle. Now, even if I could get new passes, I couldn't go with her because of my work."

★　★

Gideon said, "Maybe Emily could find another woman to go with her. Perhaps she could even be back home in time for Christmas!"

"That would be wonderful for her," Mrs. Stonum replied. "So I'll keep trying."

★ ★ ★ ★ ★

Early Sunday afternoon, after no more encounters with Levi, Nat crossed the open area from the big house to the huge kitchen. Located at a distance to help prevent the manor from catching fire, the kitchen was the undisputed domain of Aunt Hattie, the heavy-set cook. She was in her mid-forties, young for a highly valued cook. She wiped the back of her hand across her perspiring brow and scowled at him.

"Nat, why fo' y'all come so soon? Dem white folks ain't sit down to de table yet."

Nat approached where she stood before the huge fireplace. It stretched nearly across one end of the spacious room. Wonderful fragrances of spices and pork wafted from the pots and pans suspended by sturdy iron hooks over the six-foot-long pieces of blazing wood.

Nat gave her a grin and lapsed into the dialect he used around everyone except George and Delia. "Y'all sho 'nuff look powerful good today, Aunt Hattie."

She chuckled and turned away, but not before he saw a smile touch her lips. "Go 'long wit' y'all, now!" she protested, inserting a long-handled spoon into one pot and giving it a stir. "I'se got to git dis done."

Nat genuinely liked the sharp-tongued cook, who was so skilled and valuable that she even occasionally dared to look the young master or his mother in the eye. He explained, "I came to see if I could help you before—"

He broke off as Levi entered from outside. He ignored Nat to say, "Ol' woman, Massa William say he got 'portant comp'ny comin', so you be quick—"

"Git outa muh kitchen!" she interrupted, her voice rising with

★ ★

the dripping ladle she swung over her head. "Ain't you got no re-spec' fo' nothin'?"

Levi cringed and stepped back, bumping into Nat. Levi stum-bled, causing Nat to automatically reach out to help Levi recover his balance. He hurriedly left, with Aunt Hattie yelling angrily after him.

A frown furrowed Nat's brow as he watched Levi's shameful retreat. Nat told himself, *He knows better than to talk that way to her*.

Hattie's voice made Nat turn to face her. She handed him a hot hoecake. "Eat dis," she told him with feigned gruffness. "Den git outa muh way."

She tried to keep a pleased look from her face when he thanked her, picked up the prized delicacy, and enjoyed every bite. Before walking out the door, he thanked her again and dismissed Levi's strange behavior.

★ ★ ★ ★ ★

After church, Emily and Julie sat down at the long dining room table with several adult planters and others who often visited Briarstone on Sunday afternoons. Emily reminded herself to watch what she said because the guests included Mrs. Edna Weems, the outspoken widow of a Confederate colonel.

Mrs. Weems and Emily had verbally clashed months before her uncle Silas rode off to fight Yankees. While dining at Briarstone, Mrs. Weems had declared slavery was ordained by the Lord. Northern-born Emily was strongly antislavery, but she had kept quiet until pressed for her opinion. She had disagreed, which made William snap that she was excused from the table.

As she stood, William had scolded her under his breath, *"You never learn, do you?"* He was not likely to tolerate Emily's causing another such scene.

She tried to remain aloof from the inevitable discussion about what Lincoln's Emancipation Proclamation would mean to Con-federate "servants" on January first. So Emily watched the light-skinned slaves standing behind each visitor's chair. Emily observed that there was no indication in their expressions that they had

★ ★

heard a word, except for Nat. Emily caught a flicker of something in his eyes, but nobody else seemed to notice.

Mrs. Weems waved her fork in the air and spoke firmly, her multiple chins jiggling. "We have brought millions of the colored race from heathenism and rescued them from foul paganism. They should all be grateful for that and the way we care for them. Even if those terrible Yankees win the war—which they cannot—our darkies would be happy to stay and serve us as now."

Completely forgetting that she was trying to hold her tongue, Emily's indignation made her speak without thinking. "No, Mrs. Weems! If the South loses, it will be after terrible devastation! Then it would be extremely difficult for anyone to make a living, even us whites. How could freed slaves survive if they have no education, only limited skills—"

"Emily!" William's sharp word cut her off. "I think you had better excuse yourself right now!"

Anger surged through her, making her ready to defend her position. She struggled for control, knowing that she was an orphan with nowhere to go if she was forced to leave the home of her only living relatives. Glancing at Julie, Emily silently rose and rushed out of the room.

She fled into the long hallway, heading for the stairs leading to her bedchamber. She was so humiliated and angry that she didn't hear William catch up to her.

Grabbing her arm, he spun her around, his face black with rage. "I've had about enough of your impertinence," he hissed. "Embarrass me in front of guests again and you'll not be welcome here—ever! You'd have to find other accommodations and never return to Briarstone!"

He whirled around, leaving her thunderstruck but keenly aware that she had created a terrible situation.

★　★　★　★　★

Nat's face showed no reaction to William's outburst, and all the other slaves standing behind the guests' chairs appeared as though nothing had happened. Mrs. Weems loudly asked the other diners, "What did I say to distress that poor child so?"

★　★

Nat saw William's furious rush back into the room. He pushed between Mrs. Weems' chair and Delia, who stood behind it and against the wall. "Please forgive my Yankee cousin," William said, still walking but turning his face to the visitors. "She . . ."

He paused as his napkin caught on the back of the chair in front of Nat. William made an impatient motion for Nat to pick it up. As Nat bent to do so, something fell from his pocket. He watched in surprise as a small gold coin rolled across the wooden floor before stopping against Mrs. Weems' chair leg.

William didn't signal any slave to retrieve the coin, but quickly bent to pick it up. "That's my missing eagle!" he exclaimed, turning angrily to Nat.

A slave couldn't speak until spoken to, so Nat kept silent, although he was as dumbfounded as William. For a long, awkward moment, no one spoke.

Then the young master said, "Please, all of you, finish your meal. I must ask to be excused to deal with this unusual situation. Nat, follow me!"

In the hallway, William slapped Nat hard across the face.

"Thief!" he hissed, his voice low and hard.

Too startled to think clearly, Nat blurted, "But, Massa, suh, I ain't got no idee how dat—"

"Don't lie to me!" William interrupted, delivering another hard slap. "I saw it fall out of your pocket! So I've caught my thief! Come on! Let's go search your sleeping area to see what else you've taken."

Following William toward the stairwell, Nat's first sense of surprise was replaced with a harsh realization. *Levi must have stuck that coin in my pocket when he bumped into me in the kitchen!*

Nat was sure of that when William reached under the stairwell and violently yanked the sleeping pallet out into the hallway. The rustling of the corn-shuck stuffing was mixed with the sound of something hard being dragged.

"What's that?" William demanded, flipping the pallet over and touching something square inside.

Nat had no idea what that might be, but he was sure that Levi had put it there. Nat watched fearfully as the young master pulled out his jackknife and slashed the cover, exposing a book.

"My financial records!" William exclaimed, snatching the book and brushing off a corn shuck. "You're a thief!"

He protested, "Massa, I ain't never seed—"

"Don't lie, Nat!" William interrupted, his face dark with fury. "I took you back from the fields so you could work in this house again, and this is the way you thank me—by stealing! Why? You can't read. . . ."

William checked himself, his eyes narrowing in suspicion. "Or can you?"

Nat began, "Massa, I don' know how dat—"

"Don't change the subject!" William roared. "I can see the truth in your eyes: You can read! I suppose you can even speak properly, too?"

Nat kept his gaze down but did not reply.

"So I'm right!" William cried. "You're not only a thief, you're a liar trying to make a fool out of me! Well, this time I won't wait for Barley Cobb to come for you! In the morning, you're going to slave jail to be sold!"

SUDDENLY HOMELESS

Emily paced her upstairs bedchamber, too angry to throw herself across the bed and cry, yet so concerned with William's threat that she couldn't stop moving. As she strode past her window, she glanced down and saw William tying Nat to the stout whipping post in the yard.

Startled and sick at heart, Emily stopped to focus on the scene below. Only minutes before, Nat had been silently standing in place. Now Nat's wrists were secured in leather cuffs near the top of the pole.

The cuffs were so high that Nat was stretched full length, forcing him to stand on tiptoes. This painfully stretched the calf muscles while he waited for the cruel bite of the bullwhip. His bare back showed a tangled spider's web of raised scars from previous whippings.

An obviously reluctant older woman slave slowly approached with a wooden bucket. Emily had seen it all before, so she knew the bucket contained saltwater. It would be thrown on Nat's raw flesh to intensify his suffering after William finished the lashing.

Emily wondered, *What happened after I left the table?*

She expected William to take up the whip and begin using it. Instead, as the woman slave set the bucket down near the post, the young master turned away. He hurried toward the house, leaving Nat dangling from the post.

William's going back to his guests, Emily told herself. *But he'll return to whip Nat.* Emily whirled from the window and headed toward her bedchamber door. *Wait!* she warned herself, stopping to think. She had intervened once before when Nat was whipped.

If I even ask William why, she realized, *he might order me to leave Briarstone!* She couldn't risk that; not without another place to live. She returned to the window and stood looking down at Nat. *I mustn't interfere!* Emily silently repeated, closing her eyes. But she couldn't shut out the image of the cruel scars William's whip had left on Nat after the first whipping. *Think!* she told herself. *There's got to be a way to help Nat!*

★　★　★　★　★

Hanging against the post, Nat tried to ignore the ache in his arms and the muscles threatening to go into painful spasms. *I should have listened to Delia's warning about Levi,* Nat silently told himself. *He stole William's coin and his book and made sure I got blamed. Now, tied up like this, I can't even run away!*

Nat felt the cold begin seeping through his body, but nobody dared to help him. Even though slaves had free time on Sunday, and some were watching him from a distance, not one could risk offering him any comfort for fear of being punished.

Somehow, Nat told himself, dreading the coming cold of night, *I must get out of this!*

★　★　★　★　★

By nightfall, when the guests were gone and Julie had told Emily about Nat being accused of stealing the gold coin and account book, Emily approached William in the library. She asked, "May I talk to you?"

He glared at her. "What do you want?"

She spoke calmly. "Would I be interfering if I asked how much you think Nat will sell for?"

He regarded her with suspicious eyes. "It's none of your business, but with inflation, and the state just this month starting to pay owners for slaves to use against the Yankees, Nat's worth fifteen hundred dollars or more. Why do you ask?"

"Well," Emily said carefully, "if he got sick from being out in the cold all night—"

"Stop right there!" William leaped up from his chair. "That's

★　★

none of your business! I'll do what I want with my servants! Is that clear?"

Emily's calm resolve instantly evaporated. She flared, "Then you probably don't care that Nat isn't a thief, and that the real one is still going to be here in this house after Nat is sold!"

"Out! Get out!" William thrust his arm toward the open door. "I've had enough, but you won't learn. Relative or not, you're no longer welcome here. Tomorrow, get yourself another place to live!"

For a moment, Emily stood in stunned silence, but the fury in his eyes told her he meant it. "I'm sorry, William. I didn't mean to upset you."

He took a deep breath and lowered his voice. "I'm sorry it's come to this, Emily. But I really think it's time for you to move out."

"I'll start looking for a place tomorrow," Emily replied softly and walked down the hall, her mind reeling. She started up the stairs but stopped when she heard William's muffled voice.

"Levi, take a coat to Nat. Unfasten him and put him in the quarters for the night."

In spite of her own terrible problem, a faint smile touched Emily's lips as she climbed the stairs.

★　★　★　★　★

Riding in a hack with Mrs. Stonum on Monday morning, Gideon said, "Thanks for getting the doctor to let me see Zeb."

She replied, "The surgeon said maybe you can help him because the two of you had some adventures together before he joined the army. There's no doubt that he's seen too much war for a twelve-year-old, but he has to deal with his emotions if he's to get well. I pray that he'll tell you what happened."

"Me too," Gideon assured her.

She pointed. "That's Chimborazo Hospital just beyond Bloody Gulch. Over there's the James River."

Gideon studied the long rows of one-story buildings on the plateau. "It doesn't look like a hospital."

"That's what it is, though. There are over a hundred of those whitewashed buildings, and about as many army tents. With three thousand beds, this is the largest of Richmond's forty-four hospitals. Your wounded friend is in one of those smaller buildings."

"You say he was shot at Antietam?"

"Yes. On September seventeenth in Maryland. A musket went through his upper arm but missed the bone. He still got an infection, as so many wounded do. He's recovering from that but not from the emotional shock he suffered. The surgeons think that was built up over several battles until it just got to be too much for his mind to handle."

Gideon had heard that often a leg or arm wound was treated by amputation and many victims died of infection. But what had happened to Zeb's mind?

Mrs. Stonum continued, "As big as Chimborazo is, there were more than thirteen thousand of our Confederate casualties in that battle, so we were swamped. But that wasn't as bad as those days in late June and early July, when so many wounded arrived here from defending this city that there was no room in any hospital. Ambulance drivers sometimes left their patients on the streets."

Gideon remembered that Emily had been in Richmond during that time. He recalled her telling of the flies and the stench, and doctors giving patients little more than a glance to decide which wounded would be treated and which would be left to die.

Gideon promised, "I'll try to get Zeb to open up."

★   ★   ★   ★   ★

Emily awakened with a slight headache. She wasn't sure if it was from lack of sleep or losing control and weeping with Julie after she was told what William had said. Emily rose with a heavy heart, emptied water from the ceramic pitcher into the matching bowl on the bedside stand, and washed her face.

I'm almost fourteen years old and have no money and no way to earn any, she scolded herself. *I have no other relatives and no place to stay, and Christmas is coming soon. Oh, if I could just keep my opinions to myself!*

She dried her face on a small hand towel, shaking her long blond hair away from her face. *I'm sure that Mrs. Yates will help me out for a few days, but then what? At least I'm better off than Nat because I'm free, and he's going to be sold; probably into the Deep South.*

Emily absently hung the towel back on the small wall rack behind the pitcher and basin. She hurried to the window and looked down as William boarded the town coach. Nat sat on the high outside front seat with the driver, Uncle George. In a little while, Nat would be in the slave jail at Church Creek. William was so angry with him he probably wouldn't wait for the auction but have Nat sold to the first buyer who made a reasonable offer.

But fifteen hundred dollars? I don't know anyone who might buy him, unless— Again, she broke off the thought and opened the doors to her armoire. She quickly dressed, a wild possibility churning in her mind.

★ ★ ★ ★ ★

Mrs. Stonum and Gideon found Zebulon Trotter sitting up against the side of one of the whitewashed hospital buildings. He didn't even look up as the widow stopped before him.

"Zeb," she said, "look who's come to visit you."

Gideon squatted in front of Zeb. "Remember me? Gideon Tugwell? We met when we were on the road to Manassas and a Yankee soldier stole our mule."

Zeb turned dull eyes on Gideon, but there was no sign of recognition. There was only a vacant stare, as if Zeb's mind was so far away he couldn't really see them.

Gideon tried again, forcing a happy tone. "You and I had some real adventures getting that mule back. Remember?"

When Zeb's stare did not change, Gideon uncertainly looked to Mrs. Stonum.

"Keep trying," she said softly.

Nodding, Gideon shifted his gaze back to Zeb. "Do you remember when we first met? You wore ragged clothes, including a man's hat that came down over your ears. Your shoes were too big for you and the sole was coming loose. Now look at you—a real soldier all neat and clean. . . ."

Gideon's voice trailed off as he glanced at Zeb's bandaged arm

★ ★

in a sling. Quickly changing the subject, Gideon asked, "You still speak with a mountain accent?"

The faintest hint of a smile touched Zeb's lips.

Encouraged, Gideon rushed on. "I remember you told me that your parents were dead. You had run away from a mean old uncle who whipped you with a piece of rope."

Gideon hesitated, unsure if he should have mentioned that part. He added quickly, "I also remember that you told me back then, 'Don't nobody care 'bout me, not even God.' But I care about you, Zeb. I've thought of you a thousand times. You remind me of my little brother, Ben."

Gideon saw that the faint smile seemed to linger on Zeb's lips, but there was no other sign that he heard Gideon. Desperately, he plunged on. "Zeb, I know you never had a brother, but if you'll let me, I'd like to be your big brother."

Zeb made no response, causing Gideon to sigh heavily and get to his feet. He exchanged glances with Mrs. Stonum, then they turned together and started to walk away. After a couple of steps, Gideon looked back.

"I'll come to see you later, Zeb." Gideon started to turn away again but stopped as the younger boy's head slowly twisted toward the visitors. Gideon's hopes rose.

For a moment, Zeb's gray eyes lost their faraway look. He whispered, "Brother."

★ ★ ★ ★ ★

Emily borrowed one of Briarstone's four-wheeled traps and started driving toward the village of Church Creek. She felt terrible because Julie had wanted to come along, but Emily had gently yet firmly declined. That was hard because Julie was heartbroken over Emily being ordered to leave Briarstone. Yet what Emily was about to do would further anger William, and she thought it better for Julie if she didn't know anything about it.

The rural public road was usually deserted, which suited Emily. She wanted to be alone to sort out her thoughts. They were jumbled from all the ideas rolling around in her head. She faced one of the most difficult times since her parents died.

Now she was alone in the Confederacy with no money, no income, and no place to stay. She had only her faith in God, and that prompted her to do something positive about her desperate situation. But she also had another purpose in heading into the village.

She came even with the long lane that led up to the Tugwells' little farmhouse. She glanced toward it even though it was hidden behind a grove of trees. *I wonder how soon Mrs. Tugwell will hear from Gideon?*

For a moment, Emily was tempted to turn into the lane and visit, but didn't. The sooner she got to talk to Mrs. Clara Yates, the better it might be for her and Nat.

Emily's horse suddenly neighed and pointed his ears down the road. Emily looked that way and saw a black buggy top a small rise and come toward her. She guided her horse to the right, causing the four-wheeled open vehicle to slip and slide as she changed from deeper ruts to less-traveled ones. When the wheels were in the new ruts, she turned her eyes to the approaching carriage and happily cried, "Mrs. Yates!"

Moments later, the two vehicles met and stopped. Smiling, Emily said, "I was just on my way to see you!"

"Well, you found me!" the short elderly woman said with a little chuckle. She tipped her head of silvery-gray hair down to look over the top of wire-rimmed spectacles. "I was just going to call on Martha Tugwell. What can I do for you, Emily?"

"Two things," Emily replied quickly. "But I don't want to interfere with your plans."

"You won't interfere, Emily. I heard that someone has been shooting at Dilly. I want to ask about that."

"Shooting at Dilly?" Emily repeated. "The freedman who's replacing Gideon on the farm while he's away?"

"Yes. He didn't get hurt, but it makes him nervous," Mrs. Yates said. "That's only part of the scares he's had."

"Barley Cobb!" Emily exclaimed, remembering what Julie had told her. "I heard that he is trying to scare Dilly off so that—" She broke off, recalling that she was talking to the publisher of the local newspaper.

"It's all right, Emily," Mrs. Yates assured her. "I won't print what you say. Now, will you turn in here with me? I'm sure Martha won't mind."

"Well," Emily said doubtfully. "It isn't that I don't want to do that, but I need to talk privately."

"Then step over carefully and sit with me, and let's hear what's on your mind."

After cautiously making the transition to the other vehicle, Emily sat beside the older woman and looked into her warm, friendly blue eyes.

"William accused his former body slave, Nat, of being a thief and has sent him to slave jail to be sold. I know he's innocent, but if he's sold into the Deep South, he'll probably die young and never have a chance for freedom again!"

Mrs. Yates didn't seem surprised. "I'm guessing that you hope I'll buy Nat and manumit him?"

Emily blinked at the woman's keen perception. "I know I have no right to even mention this," Emily added quickly, "but you and your husband once helped him escape on the Underground Railroad. Even if he escaped again, he wouldn't really be free because William will put Barley Cobb on his trail. But if Nat's freedom was bought—"

Mrs. Yates broke in. "I understand. Now, what's your second reason for wanting to see me?"

She took a deep breath before replying. "William again ordered me off the place and told me to never come back, so I need your advice on where I can find a place to stay in exchange for doing some work."

For a long moment, the older woman didn't speak. Then she smiled. "Emily, I believe I know just the right person—Mrs. Ada Wheeler. Like you, she's originally from Illinois. I'll arrange for you to meet her."

Emily's hopes soared, but she warned herself, *Don't count your chickens before they hatch!*

THE SLAVE JAIL

For the first full day after he arrived at the slave jail, Nat was the only occupant inside. He was shoved into a small room where the only light came from a tiny window interlaced with heavy iron bars. The dreary place was filled with foul smells and a hint of something so intangible that Nat seemed to feel it more than detect it with his five senses.

Hopelessness, he decided. *I can't touch, taste, hear, see, or smell it, but that's what it is. When all hope is gone, it must create a sensation that is so strong it seeps into the walls from all the poor slaves confined here.*

For a moment, Nat was tempted to yield to the same feeling but was comforted by remembering his mother's often-repeated philosophy, *"Winning is in the mind. . . ."* He also recalled something Uncle George had said about how he was able to graciously bear a slave's life. *"It's the way I look at things, Nat,"* the old carriage driver had confided. *"The earth isn't my real home; I'm just passing through. Faith gives me a glory inside. I try to show that outside by the way I live."*

Attitude, Nat mused. *The way to look at things. Even though I'm about to be unjustly sold to the Deep South, I mustn't give up hope.*

He raised his dark eyes to the gloomy ceiling, trying by faith to see beyond it. Somewhat cheered, Nat shuffled across the cell toward the light, restrained by a three-foot link of chain connecting both ankles. He clutched the window bars with manacled wrists. These in turn were attached to a chain around his waist.

These had been placed on him by the white jailer after William warned that Nat was a repeat runaway.

A soft voice spoke from the gloomy adjacent cell. "Ain't no good to look out dere, boy. Even if'n y'all gits out de doah, dey gots a big wall pas' dat. You an' me, we daid, only we cain't jis' lay down and die proper."

A little startled at realizing he wasn't alone, Nat turned to probe the dimness with anxious eyes. Then he realized that the other slave must have been brought in while Nat slept fitfully on the filthy corn-shuck mattress.

As Nat's eyes adjusted to the change from the brightness outside the window to the shadowy cell, he made out a small man peering through his bars.

Nat was too busy wondering how he might escape before he was sold to be conversational, but he needed any information he could get about this place. He asked, "We de only ones heah?"

"Sho 'nuff. De auction was two days back. All gone but you'n me. My massa say I stole his finger ring. You?"

Nat decided not to try explaining the unfairness of his situation. "Same, only it was a book."

The other man chuckled. "A book! Ain't dat some'm? Well, we bof' gwine be sold down de ribber."

The sound of a key turning in the heavy iron door made Nat turn that direction. The huge bulk of the jailer filled the door. "Hey, boy . . . Nat, or whatever they call you. Step out. You've been sold."

Nat involuntarily twitched in shock but didn't stir.

"Move!" the jailer commanded, pulling a short club from his belt and thumping it against his open left palm.

"Yassa," Nat replied and shuffled forward to whatever unknown new master awaited him.

★ ★ ★ ★ ★

After visiting with Gideon's mother while Clara Yates questioned her about the mysterious shots fired in Dilly's direction, Emily was deeply concerned. It wasn't just the sound of musket balls whistling by his ears that worried Dilly, according to what he told Mrs. Tugwell.

There had been strange and mysterious sounds in the night when he went outside alone, leaving John Fletcher asleep in the barn where they shared quarters. Like many of his people, Dilly was superstitious and deathly afraid of "hain'ts," or haunts. Mrs. Tugwell had not succeeded in convincing Dilly that there were no such things, even in the adjacent swamp.

The conversation eventually drifted around to the story of Nat's being jailed and Emily's being forced to leave Briarstone. Mrs. Tugwell promptly offered to take Emily in for a while, but she politely declined. The little Tugwell house with its lean-to bedroom was already so full that both Fletcher and Dilly slept in the barn. With winter coming, they would soon need a stove out there, and there was no money for that. Emily didn't have any money, either, and the family certainly didn't need another person to feed.

Mrs. Yates had asked if she might speak to Fletcher privately. Mrs. Tugwell told the visitor she would find him in the barn. While Mrs. Yates was gone, Emily learned that Gideon's mother hoped to soon hear from him. Emily sensed the unspoken concern that the mother had for her son alone in the big city.

Mrs. Yates returned, saying, "Martha, I hope you don't mind, but I asked Mr. Fletcher to run an urgent errand for me. There wasn't time to ask you properly."

Mrs. Tugwell's eyebrows arched in surprise, but she nodded. "Of course, Clara."

Moments later, Emily saw Fletcher ride the family mule down the lane toward the public road.

★　★　★　★　★

Afterward, riding with Mrs. Yates on the way into the village to meet Mrs. Wheeler, Emily glanced back to make sure her borrowed horse and trap were still tied to the back of the buggy. Satisfied, she faced Mrs. Yates.

"I'm concerned about what might happen to Dilly."

Mrs. Yates replied, "I'm concerned, too. But there are no witnesses to prove that Cobb's responsible for those shots. In fact,

Dilly, John Fletcher, Martha, and Martha's children have never even seen Cobb around there since she ordered him to stay away. Without proof, nothing can be done to him."

Emily protested, "But if Cobb succeeds in scaring Dilly off, then Mrs. Tugwell will have no choice but to ask Gideon to come home. Mr. Fletcher is a very hard worker, but he can't do all the work with only one hand."

"And that," Mrs. Yates added, "would severely delay Gideon's dream of becoming a writer in Richmond. It's too bad that Martha's stepson is off fighting the Federals. Isham loves farming as much as Gideon hates it."

Emily replied, "It would be worse if Cobb and William succeed in running Dilly off and Gideon's mother loses the farm. That's the only way they have of making a living. I wish I could help, but I don't know anything about farming."

"Even if you did, my dear, it takes physical strength that you and I don't have. But we mustn't lose hope for them."

"Oh, I won't!" Emily assured her. "But I want so much to have Gideon succeed as a writer. He and the family are risking everything to achieve that dream."

"I know." Mrs. Yates turned to face Emily. "What about you? What are your dreams?"

"Except for getting home to Illinois, I don't have any other special things I want." A wave of homesickness swept over Emily, almost overwhelming her. "It would be so wonderful to be there for Christmas. Jessie Barlow, my best friend, and I would have such a good time. Well . . ."

Emily left her thought unfinished as memories of her late family flashed into her mind. The homesickness was so severe, she had to force her mind away from Illinois.

Mrs. Yates said, "Before we get to Mrs. Wheeler's home, I want to ask you a question, Emily. All right?"

"Of course."

"Have you ever heard about Cleobulus?"

"No. Who's he?"

"He was the king of Rhodes and considered the wisest of the wise. He said something that I think you should think about."

★ ★

"What's that?"

Smiling, Mrs. Yates replied, "That's Ada's place ahead. I'll have to tell you after we talk with her."

Emily's curiosity was aroused, but she quickly refocused her thoughts to Ada Wheeler. *I hope she's a nice woman,* Emily told herself, *and she'll take me in for a while until I figure out how to get out of my situation.*

★ ★ ★ ★ ★

After hearing Zeb utter the single word *brother,* Gideon decided to stay with Zeb after the widow left. As Gideon kept talking, he eagerly waited for more responses from Zeb. He didn't say another word, although Gideon sensed that Zeb's mind seemed to be trying to return from whatever faraway place it had escaped to. The vacant staring into space sometimes changed, and occasionally his eyes followed Gideon as he rambled on.

He spoke about many incidents he could recall from his and Zeb's previous encounter, but he mentioned nothing about their experience following the First Battle of Manassas. Gideon knew that the twelve-year-old boy had seen too much of death and wounds since then, so Gideon tried to give a humorous twist to some of their episodes.

It soon became exhausting because Zeb didn't respond beyond the occasional shifting of his gaze. He didn't speak. Gideon wasn't even sure Zeb was really listening.

Finally, more emotionally drained than he thought possible, Gideon stopped his chatter. Reluctantly, he rose and looked down at the younger boy.

"Zeb, I have to go away for a while, but I'll come back. When I do, I'll let you do the talking and I'll listen. Fair enough?"

Gideon watched Zeb's eyes, hoping they would lose their faraway look and focus on him. When they didn't, and there was no reaction, Gideon took a deep breath and repeated, "I'll be back later, Zeb."

★ ★ ★ ★ ★

The jailer removed the last chain from Nat and motioned him

★ ★

through a door into a small office. It smelled of sweat, unemptied spittoons, and something that Nat thought would be fear, if fear had a smell.

He recognized John Fletcher at once, but when the one-handed man gave no indication of knowing Nat, he dropped his eyes and pretended he had never seen his benefactor before.

The jailer said to Fletcher, "Don't say I didn't warn you if he runs off from you. You can take a look at his back and see how he's been whupped before for that. Only he don't seem to never learn."

"He won't run from me," Fletcher said in his soft Southern accent.

With peripheral vision from his downcast eyes, Nat watched the jailer glance at Fletcher's left wrist, where he had lost a hand at Manassas. "Mister," the jailer said, "I sure hope you got a pistol in case he—"

"I told you, he won't run," Fletcher interrupted. He turned to Nat. "Let's go."

Nat followed in silence, still too surprised to figure out what this was all about. He knew that Fletcher was a hired hand at the Tugwells', where he worked for room and board, without wages. Mrs. Tugwell obviously had no extra money, so Nat's purchase price hadn't come from her.

Outside, Nat lifted his head and took in the grand sight of open sky from horizon to horizon. Sucking in a great gulp of fresh air, Nat closed his eyes in a blissful moment of being free of the foul jail. His eyes popped open when he heard Fletcher's voice.

"Riding double is the only transportation I can offer you."

Nat grinned, aware that Fletcher knew he could speak proper English. "Riding double right now sounds great," Nat declared. "Where are we going?"

"To meet your benefactor. You want to ride in front or back?"

"Either is fine," Nat replied, a slight frown creasing his brow. "Who's my benefactor?"

Fletcher swung into the saddle and turned to motion for Nat to get up behind him. "Mrs. Clara Yates."

This second surprise hit Nat so hard that he didn't try to

★ ★

mount but gawked at Fletcher. "But she doesn't have slaves any-more! She freed all of . . . Oh!"

The realization of what might be happening struck Nat with the force of a blow. "Oh!" he said again.

Fletcher grinned down at him. "You going to stand there or ride with me?"

"Ride with you!" Nat cried and joyfully leaped up to sit behind Fletcher.

★　★　★　★　★

Mrs. Ada Wheeler walked around her large, open kitchen with her head thrust forward, emphasizing the humped and rounded shoulders. She had arthritic fingers that curled but could not close properly. This caused her cane to occasionally slip from her grasp. But her hazel eyes were bright and her smile as cheerful as if she had no health problems at all.

"So, Emily," she said after they had sipped buttermilk at the unadorned wooden table, "what do you think? Do we have an agreement?"

"You're more than generous," Emily replied. "And I am happy to accept your hospitality until I can make permanent arrange-ments."

Mrs. Wheeler beamed. "It'll be good to hear a young voice in the house again."

Mrs. Yates commented, "I thought you two would get along famously."

Emily told her, "I'm grateful to you for getting Mrs. Wheeler and me together."

Mrs. Yates smiled. "I'm glad it worked out."

Ada Wheeler told Emily, "I envy you because you still have this dream of returning to your Illinois home. I would dearly love to see my only living sister in Chicago. But I'm afraid my traveling days are over."

Emily wondered if Mrs. Wheeler meant she would probably die before the war ended and the lines opened again. *Or maybe*, Emily thought, glancing at the crippled fingers and the cane, *she means those.*

Mrs. Wheeler noticed where Emily's eyes rested. "Oh," the woman explained. "I didn't mean because of these." She briefly lifted the gnarled hands and the cane. "I could go anywhere this way if it weren't for this awful war. But I can't get passes through the military lines."

Emily nodded, recalling the long struggle she had had to obtain the precious passes, only to have them expire when she and Mrs. Stonum were delayed at the Second Battle of Manassas.

Mrs. Wheeler changed topics. "Tell me, Emily," she said, "what do you plan to do when you're grown?"

"I don't know yet. Probably do like most girls, I guess. Get married, have a family, that sort of thing."

Mrs. Yates shook her head. "Emily, a newspaper person learns many things about lots of people. I have watched you for more than a year, and I think you have a most remarkable talent."

"I do?"

"Yes, you do. In fact, I have previously mentioned this to Ada on various occasions. Right, Ada?"

"Oh yes," she agreed. "Emily, from all Clara has told me, and from talking to you this last hour or so, I believe she's right."

"Right about what?" Emily asked, perplexed.

The two women exchanged glances before Mrs. Yates answered. "Remember on the ride over here when I asked if you had ever heard of Cleobulus?"

The girl nodded. "Yes, you said he was king of Rhodes, considered a very wise man, and had said something that you thought I should think about."

"Well, perhaps now's the time to finish that story."

Puzzled, Emily fixed her eyes on Mrs. Yates and asked, "Now I'm very curious. What did he say?"

The women looked at each other, then spoke in unison: " 'Educate the children.' "

They said nothing more but looked at Emily with big smiles as if they were both delighted with that quote.

Emily was mystified. "I . . . I don't understand."

"You will," Mrs. Yates assured her.

Emily leaned forward to hear the explanation.

★ ★

FREEDOM IS NOT FREE

As the mule carrying double left the village, Nat asked Fletcher, "Where're we going?"

"To the Tugwells' farm. Mrs. Yates told me to take you there until her husband could come for you."

Nat fearfully asked, "Do you think they bought me to set me free as she and her husband already did with their slaves? Or is she going to keep slaves again and I'm one of them?"

"I don't know," Fletcher replied.

"May I ask how much she paid for me?"

Fletcher hesitated before replying, "Fifteen hundred dollars. The trader wanted more, but Mrs. Yates had told me to mention that you'd run away twice. So the jailer lowered the price."

Nat's eyes opened wide. As a slave he had never owned a cent, but he had often heard white folks talking about money. They had said a government clerk in Richmond only made twelve hundred a year. If Mrs. Yates had not bought him as a slave, he would owe her his full purchase price. Even as a freedman, hired out for wages, it would take years to repay fifteen hundred dollars.

Fletcher continued, "Mrs. Yates was at the Tugwells' when she asked me to saddle up and take a note to her husband, saying it was urgent and that she would explain to Mrs. Tugwell. I found Mr. Yates on his farm, where he read her note."

When Fletcher paused, Nat prompted, "And?"

"And he went into his house and came out with cash wrapped in a package. He told me I was to take it to the jail and buy you. If I was asked where I got the money, I wasn't to tell. I guess they didn't want it known that they had anything to do with this. So you'll have to wait for answers to your questions."

Nat knew that was true, but it didn't ease his anxiety and concern about his purchase price.

★ ★ ★ ★ ★

Mrs. Yates explained to Emily, "Cleobulus was among the famous Seven Sages of ancient Greece. There's a story about a merchant who made a deal with a fisherman for whatever his next net brought up. Instead of fish, it held a golden tripod, which is like a kettle on three legs. The merchant claimed it was his, but the fisherman disputed that. So to settle the issue, the story says that the oracle at Delphi was consulted, and he said the tripod should be given to the wisest of the wise."

Emily didn't know about the oracle at Delphi or the Seven Sages. "I still don't understand," she said.

"You will," Mrs. Yates assured her. "Every wise man consulted had a different answer about the tripod, none of which really seemed to have anything to do with the question. Yet some of their advice is still quoted today as old sayings. One was, 'Whatever you do, do it well.' But Cleobulus's quote about educating the children isn't nearly as well-known."

Emily frowned, still confused.

Her new landlady said, "Clara, I do believe that for a newspaper publisher you aren't making yourself clear."

"I'm coming to that, Ada. Now, Emily, Ada and I have often talked about what will happen to the four million slaves when this war is over and they're all free."

Emily asked, "You think the South's going to lose the war?"

"If I said that," Mrs. Yates replied with a wry smile, "I might be considered a traitor, so I'm just asking a hypothetical question."

"Everyone knows I'm a Yankee," Emily said. "So I could ask that question, and I did. I asked William and some of his friends. That stirred up a hornet's nest."

Mrs. Yates chuckled. "I would expect that. Southern planters don't want to even consider that the Union might win this war.

★ ★

But both Ada and I like to look ahead and contemplate what might possibly happen."

Mrs. Wheeler spoke eagerly, apparently concerned that her friend was too slow in getting to the point. "Some time ago, Emily, Clara told me how you helped a boy named Gideon to read, write, and spell better. And—"

"And," Mrs. Yates broke in, "I also told her how you taught Briarstone's overseer's children to read, and that some of the little slave youngsters stood around and listened. Of course, it's against the law to make them literate, but they're obviously hungry to learn to read and write. That's when your name came up."

Mrs. Wheeler blurted, "We think you could become a school-teacher!"

Emily blinked. "What?"

"Yes!" Mrs. Yates said. "When the war is over, you could not only educate white children, but those of slaves who will then be free! What do you think?"

Emily gawked at both women in total surprise.

"Oh," Mrs. Wheeler cried, "we're not asking you to make such a decision now."

"Of course not," Mrs. Yates agreed. "We just want you to think about it. There's going to be a tremendous need for teachers when this war is over. So many men are dead or going to be killed on both sides that there won't be enough of them left to teach all the children. That means women must become educators!"

"Whoever teaches in the South," Mrs. Wheeler said, "will have to care about all students, regardless of color."

"I've always enjoyed teaching children," Emily admitted, "beginning when I taught Sunday school in Illinois. But if I did consider teaching school, I'd do that in Illinois, where I still plan to go, hopefully before Christmas."

"My dear Emily," Mrs. Yates said, "teaching is one of the spiritual gifts mentioned in the Bible. I believe you have that gift. I also believe God has a plan for every life, and you do have a talent for teaching."

"I don't know . . ." Emily began.

"Will you at least pray about it?" Mrs. Yates asked.

★ ★

Emily fell silent as she considered how to answer.

★　★　★　★　★

Knowing he had to meet Herb Hunter to start the courier job, Gideon walked away from Chimborazo toward the center of Richmond. *It hurts me to see Zeb like that*, Gideon silently admitted. *What awful thing happened to make him draw inside himself?*

Continuing toward the capitol, Gideon's mind jumped again, visualizing his tired mother, his young brother, Ben, and sisters, Kate and Lilly. *I hope everything is all right with them*, he thought. *And I hope that Dilly is working out so he and Mr. Fletcher are handling all the hard work without me.*

A tinge of homesickness touched Gideon. He shook his head to dislodge the feeling. *I'd better write Mama and let her know I'm all right. And Emily; I'd better drop her a note, too.*

He tried to keep from thinking about Zeb, but it was no use. *Mrs. Stonum says he's got to talk about whatever happened in the war if he's going to get well. As soon as I can, I'll be back to try again.*

★　★　★　★　★

Nat had never been on the Tugwells' property until Fletcher turned Hercules off the public road onto the long lane leading up to the tiny house. Nat stiffened in alarm when two hounds charged down the lane with long ears flapping and deep voices baying.

Goose bumps of fear erupted on Nat's arms as he vividly remembered more than a year ago when Barley Cobb's vicious hounds had bayed on his and a slave girl's trail. He and Sarah had run away from Briarstone and into the swamp behind the Tugwell farm in a desperate bid for freedom. They had eluded Cobb's dogs, but the frightening memory was coupled with countless stories Nat had heard of runaway slaves being horribly mauled by hounds. Especially the hounds trained to trail only slaves.

Fletcher said, "They won't hurt you." He spoke firmly to the hounds. "Rock! Red! Quiet!"

The dogs obeyed, circling around in back of Hercules as he plodded up to the house. Nat kept his eyes on the dogs, unsure of

★　★

what they would do when he dismounted.

The front door opened, and a white woman stepped out onto the small porch and waved in greeting.

"That's Gideon's mother," Fletcher explained, stopping Hercules. "I'm sure Mrs. Yates told her to expect you. You can step down and go meet her while I put the mule back in the barn."

Nat hesitated, peering apprehensively down at the dogs. "Uh . . . I could help with the mule."

Fletcher smiled knowingly. "I should have thought of that. Why don't I ground-hitch Hercules right here so you and I can go into the house together?" He dismounted without waiting for an answer.

Nat slid to the ground, keeping a wary eye on the dogs while wondering why Mrs. Yates had him brought here.

★   ★   ★   ★   ★

Gideon met Herb Hunter where he waited with two saddle horses in front of the *Sentinel*. "Sorry I'm a little late," Gideon apologized. "Mrs. Stonum took me to see my friend Zeb, but he didn't seem to recognize me. So I stayed awhile longer, trying to get him to talk."

"A good newspaper correspondent keeps trying," Hunter replied approvingly. "You ride much?"

Gideon eyed the horses with some trepidation. "Only our old mule for short distances."

Swinging into the saddle, Hunter replied, "It's been a long time since I rode horseback. I rented these two from the livery stable. They're faster than a buggy. I just hope we don't run into any soldiers who need the horses more than we do."

Gideon also mounted, asking, "You mean Yankees?"

"Not necessarily. Horses are getting so scarce that even some of our own troops are 'requisitioning' any animals they want. In war, that's not considered theft."

That information made Gideon somewhat anxious as Hunter turned his mount and started down the street. Gideon moved his horse up beside the other. "What do we do if somebody takes our horses?"

"We walk," Hunter said with a grin. "But let's not borrow trouble. Instead, tell me more about your friend."

"There's not much to tell," Gideon replied but recited details of his visits with Zeb.

When he finished, Hunter said, "If you can get him to tell you what happened, maybe you could write his story. If Kerr likes it, he'll pay you stringer rates. That means for the total printed inches you write."

Gideon admitted, "I hadn't thought of that. Besides, I'm not sure I can write well enough yet."

"You write it the best you can, Gideon, and I'll look it over for you and make any suggested changes."

Gideon's self-doubt made him ask, "What if it's really bad writing?"

"I don't think anyone who wants to write as much as you do would write something that couldn't be fixed. So stop worrying and think how you can write Zeb's story so well Kerr will be glad to run it."

Gideon gave Hunter a grateful smile. "Thanks."

"Whoa!" Hunter suddenly stopped his horse and turned toward Gideon. "We've got a little time before I have to report back to my regiment. Why don't you take me over to the hospital to meet Zeb?"

"Good idea!" Gideon replied, turning his mount around. "Maybe you can break through Zeb's silence."

★　★　★　★　★

Nat was relieved when Gideon's mother and her three younger children treated him as a welcome visitor. It was difficult for Nat to sit and drink buttermilk with white people, and it was even harder to wait for answers to the questions buzzing in his head.

Ben, Kate, and Lilly regarded him with solemn eyes as Mrs. Tugwell said, "Nat, I'm sure you're very anxious to have Mrs. Yates return and answer all your questions. But I guess it's all right for me to tell you what she said before she left."

Fletcher returned from putting Hercules away as Mrs. Tugwell

★　★

turned to the children. "Please go outside and play. Let me know when Mrs. Yates arrives."

The youngsters left protesting, with twelve-year-old Ben wisely pointing out, "The hounds will do that." Still, at his mother's motion, he followed his sisters out the back door just as the two dogs suddenly burst out from under the back porch. They raced around the house, bawling loudly to announce that someone was coming.

Nat noticed Mrs. Tugwell and Fletcher exchange glances before she headed for the front window, saying over her shoulder, "John, if it's Barley Cobb again . . ."

Nat didn't hear the rest because mentioning Cobb sent a shock through him. He leaped to his feet, his heart racing at memories of his experiences with the brutal slave catcher and his hounds.

Mrs. Tugwell said from the window, "It's Clara Yates. Now you'll get the answers to your questions."

★　★　★　★　★

Nat's benefactor greeted him warmly and smiled when he thanked her for buying him from the slave jail. Aware that Nat knew Emily, the newspaper publisher told about Emily going to stay awhile with Ada Wheeler after William ordered her to leave Briarstone and never return.

"I'm very sorry to hear that," Nat said earnestly. "I'm partly to blame for that because she defended me more than once. I'm really very, very sorry."

"She'll be all right," Mrs. Yates declared. "My friend Ada and I suggested she become a schoolteacher after the war. But her only dream now is to get back home to Illinois, preferably in time for Christmas."

"I hope she makes it," Nat said.

Mrs. Yates cleared her throat. "Speaking of Emily's dreams, Nat, Gideon is in Richmond trying to make his writing dream come true. I think I can guess yours."

Nat gulped. *Here it comes!* he thought.

Mrs. Yates continued, "It will take some time for all the legal paper work to be completed, Nat, but my husband and I are manumitting you. We'll have to go to the courthouse, get the proper forms, have them filled in and signed with the help of an attorney, then wait for the judicial process to be completed. Eventually, it'll be final, and you'll be a freedman."

Although not totally unexpected, the realization of what she meant seized Nat hard. *I'll be free! A freedman! Not a runaway slave trying to reach Canada and liberty, but legally manumitted to full independence of any master! I can try to find either of my brothers without listening for hounds on my trail!*

Nat tried to thank her, but no words came. His mouth moved, but his emotion was too great for words.

"It's all right," Mrs. Yates assured him, her blue eyes sparkling with shiny, unshed tears. "I understand your feelings. But you should be aware that even as a legally free person, you will still be in danger."

A slight frown touched Nat's forehead. "How so?"

"William will be furious when he finds out," Mrs. Yates explained. "He can't harm me, but he might have Barley Cobb try to kidnap you and sell you back into slavery far from here!"

★ ★

THE WAR
BALLOON

For a moment, Mrs. Yates's dire warning yanked Nat's memory back to his first escape from Briarstone. He recalled his desperate run through the swamp with the slave girl Sarah. In his mind, Nat could hear Cobb's hounds baying as they closed in. Closer, closer...

Stop it! Nat silently rebuked himself. *Think about freedom! Freedom!* The word gave wings to Nat's spirit.

I can soon go anywhere! Instead of my having to run away and find my little brother Amos and escape together to Canada, maybe I could buy his freedom just as the Yateses bought mine. But before I can do that, somehow I have to repay the fifteen hundred dollars my freedom cost them.

Mrs. Yates told him, "You'll be safer if you work with my husband on the farm until your papers are completed. You'll be paid a fair wage. Then, when you're legally free, you should get far away from this place as quickly as possible."

All his life, Nat had been taught to never look a white person in the eye. Now he raised his, looking into the eyes of Fletcher, Mrs. Tugwell, and then Mrs. Yates.

"I am very grateful to all of you," he began, "and to your husband, Mrs. Yates. More than I can say."

He spoke with hidden meaning that he hoped she alone would understand. He doubted that anyone except Emily and he knew that Mr. and Mrs. Yates were local "conductors" on the secret Underground Railroad. More than a year ago, with Emily, they had helped him and Sarah escape after eluding Cobb's hounds in the swamp. Sarah had made it to Canada, but Nat had been caught and returned to William.

"But," Nat continued, still looking at Mrs. Yates, "even at the risk from Barley Cobb, I can't leave without repaying what my freedom cost you and your husband."

"Thank you for saying that," she replied, "but when you're a freedman, if you wish, you can hire out for wages in some faraway place. Send us whatever you can over a period of years."

Years! The word echoed in Nat's mind. How long will it take to repay fifteen hundred dollars?

Aloud he said, "Thank you, Mrs. Yates." Nat turned to Gideon's mother and Fletcher. "Thank you, too. I have run from slavery and been in great danger, so I will not run from freedom, no matter how great the peril. Do you all understand?"

All three adults slowly nodded.

*   *   *   *   *

Emily returned the borrowed horse to Briarstone, where Julie tearfully helped her pack her belongings. Handing Emily's hairbrush and comb to her, Julie exclaimed, "I'm going to miss you so terribly much!"

Emily fought to control the hot moisture forming in her own eyes. She dropped the items into her carpetbag and hugged Julie. "I'll miss you, too. You made life much easier for me while I lived here."

"I tried to get William to change his mind," Julie said brokenly, "but he wouldn't listen."

"Thanks for trying, but it's time for me to move on. Never forget that I'll always love you very much."

"As much as your friend Jessie in Illinois?"

The question surprised Emily. She said thoughtfully, "Jessie and I have been best friends since we were little girls. You and I weren't always friends because we lived in different states. But in the time I've lived here, I have come to love you far more than as just a cousin. Now we will always love each other as very special friends."

Julie broke into greater weeping, her body racked with convulsive sobs. Emily held her close, saying nothing, until the tears slowed and Julie broke the embrace.

Julie brushed her moist cheeks with a forefinger. "I don't know why we're carrying on so! We'll see each other at church and in the village."

"William wouldn't appreciate seeing me in church. I'll attend where Mrs. Wheeler and the Tugwells do."

"That makes me very sad, but I understand," Julie said. "Speaking of them, I wonder how Gideon is doing?"

"So do I. I'll write him with my new address." Emily looked around the room. "Well, I guess that's everything. If William will let Uncle George drive me over to Mrs. Wheeler's, I'll say good-bye to everyone and be on my way."

"I'll drive!" Julie stooped to pick up the carpetbag. "Since William ordered you off of Briarstone, I'm sure he won't object if I take you over in the buggy."

"Oh, thank you, Julie! There's something else I'd like to talk to you about, but I didn't want to get into a discussion here. I can tell you about it on the ride."

★   ★   ★   ★   ★

Topping another Richmond hill, Gideon pointed from the saddle. "That's Chimborazo over there."

"I've been there," Hunter replied, "but fortunately never as a patient."

Gideon's eyes swept to the right down toward the James River. He blinked and pointed again. "What's that?"

"That's the Confederate Navy Yard."

"No, I mean that thing that looks like a giant ball tied down with lots of ropes to the deck of that ship."

"Oh, that's a Confederate war balloon."

"War balloon?" Gideon asked.

"Actually," Hunter explained, "it's the army's aerial observation balloon. It's raised up in the sky with ropes to a height of a couple hundred feet. A soldier rides in a wicker basket underneath the bag part so he can spy on Union positions. Information from the balloon is relayed to our commanders, who then better know how to deploy our forces."

"Why is it there on a ship's deck?"

"Two reasons. Sometimes the balloon is towed on a railroad car to where it's needed. Other times, it's carried up or down the river on a ship. The other reason it's here is because ordinary city gas is used to fill the balloon and make it rise. The Lower Gas Works plant is right over there between Bloody Run and Poplar Streets, this side of the dock area. In the first balloon they used hot air, but gas works better."

"Oh!" Gideon cried, standing in the stirrups. "I want to see it up close! Could we go down there?"

Hunter hesitated. "Well, I guess we can take a few minutes. But they won't let us get too close, so we'll have to tie our horses and walk as far as we can."

Gideon excitedly turned his horse toward the site.

★ ★ ★ ★ ★

Regardless of how bravely Nat had spoken about not running away because of Barley Cobb's likely action, he was tense as he rode in the buggy with Mrs. Yates.

She seemed to sense that. "We'll soon be at the farm, where you'll be under my husband's watchful eye."

Nat said, "I hope he's not going to be in any danger because of buying my freedom."

"Oh no. William is young and immature in many ways, but he's also quite intelligent. He would not dare harm either my husband or me. But you must watch out when you're off alone where Cobb might try to snatch you."

"I'll be careful."

"Of course, if anything did happen to you, William and Cobb would both deny having any involvement, so the only way to protect yourself is to do as I've suggested."

Nat nodded without answering. His eyes swept the public road and the landscape in every direction. Trees clustered together like islands in a sea of cultivated lands. It had not rained for a few days, but the clouds hung menacingly on the horizon. Nat took a great gulp of the crisp autumn air.

"Freedom!" he said softly, savoring the word. "This is what freedom looks and smells like!"

His benefactress told him, "Enjoy it, Nat. You've been denied it all these years, but many of your fellow slaves will never draw a free breath."

Nodding, Nat thought of Uncle George and Delia. "But I hope my brother will," Nat mused. "I not only want to make enough to repay you and your husband, but enough to buy Amos's freedom."

"Your brother?"

"Yes, one of two still missing. I've heard that Amos is in bondage on a small farm near here. My mother, three little brothers, and a sister were all separated when our first master died and the heirs sold us off. As you know, after William bought me I ran away twice and found my mother, sister, and one brother. I got caught both times after I escaped from Briarstone, but I did help all three of them to escape to Canada. Now that I'm free, I—"

He broke off suddenly. "Sorry, Mrs. Yates. I guess I'm so excited that I'm talking too much."

"I like to hear you talk, Nat. In fact, I have something in mind to ask you about. But first, have you ever thought about what you would do if you were truly free?"

"All I ever wanted to do was find my family so we could all be together again."

"Of course. That's a very noble ambition. But you're facing young manhood as a free person, so what would you like to do if you could be or do *anything* you wanted?"

A sad smile touched his lips. "A slave doesn't ever dream much beyond being free."

"I suppose. But now that you can, I hope you'll think about it. Will you?"

"Certainly. But I don't have a single idea now," Nat admitted.

"Take your time. Meanwhile, I have another question. Will you talk to a small group of my friends about your life as a slave?"

Nat had to control a strong desire to violently shake his head. Speak to a group of white women? The idea was frightening. *Yet I owe her so much*, Nat told himself.

He stalled, then asked, "Could I have some time to think about it?"

"Of course. But if I'm right, in the long run it may open your eyes to something I'm sure you've never even dreamed about."

She left silently, leaving Nat to ponder what she could mean.

★ ★ ★ ★ ★

The only sound in the buggy was the steady rise and fall of the horses' hooves in the public road after Emily told Julie about the suggestion she someday become a schoolteacher.

Finally Julie said thoughtfully, "A teacher. I don't know about that. First, I don't think the South is going to lose the war. But if I'm wrong, and Lincoln frees all those slaves, it's going to be such a huge mess that no amount of teachers or teaching could make a difference."

"I didn't mean I would come back here to teach!" Emily exclaimed. "That was their idea. But in the short time since they mentioned it, I've silently prayed about it. I like teaching, but it's a man's job."

"Unfortunately," Julie said with a heavy sigh, "those women are right about there going to be a shortage of men when this cruel war is over."

"Oh, I still would never come back to the South!" Emily vehemently declared. "If the Confederacy is beaten, there will be intense bitterness toward anyone from the Union who came down here."

"No matter how the war ends," Julie said, "there's going to be bitterness on both sides."

"I'm sure you're right," Emily agreed, "but if the Union wins, life would be miserable for any Yankee who dared to come here. Southern feelings would be even more harsh toward anyone, man or woman, if they tried to teach black children. So even if I did decide to teach school, it would only be in the North."

Julie commented, "I wish we could live near each other when we're grown-up and this mess is over."

"I'd like that, too," Emily admitted. "But when I can, I'm going

★ ★

back to Illinois to stay. I'd really love to be there in time for Christmas. I'd go caroling with Jessie and . . . uh . . . others again."

Julie looked sharply at Emily. "Jessie and her big brother, you mean?"

A hint of color touched Emily's cheeks because she had told Julie about Brice Barlow twice saying he was going to marry Emily when she grew up. "Brice is off somewhere fighting for the Union. He won't be home."

"Probably not, but you were thinking about him just now, weren't you?"

Emily hadn't consciously done that, but his image floated into her mind. Tall, good-looking, with that gentle teasing way in which he had always treated her. He would be nineteen or twenty now, she decided.

Julie asked, "What about Gideon?"

"He's a friend, like Brice."

"You're old enough to have a beau," Julie reminded her. "Lots of girls are married when they're sixteen. So if you had to choose a beau, which would it be: Brice or Gideon?"

Evasively, Emily suggested, "Let's go back to the schoolteacher idea. What do you think I should do?"

"Don't ask me," Julie replied. "Ask the Lord."

Emily didn't like that answer. She had already made up her mind. This was not something she wanted to pray about—not even once.

★　★　★　★　★

Leaving their horses tied to a street post, Gideon and Hunter continued toward the port area. "It's so big!"

"Certainly is," Hunter agreed. "It's about seventy-five cubic feet."

"It's also so pretty and shiny!" Gideon exclaimed, his eyes on the observation balloon. "Like a rich lady's dress I saw in a window shop in downtown Richmond."

"For good reason," Hunter replied. "It's called the 'Silk Dress Balloon' because it's made of silk. Many people believe Confederate ladies donated their silk dresses for the project, but that's not true."

"It looks as if that's what it could be."

"It was cut from a huge bolt of cloth with what's called a trefoil design," Hunter said. "I know because I wrote a story about war balloons for the *Sun* some time ago. The bag is made airtight by varnishing the silk pattern. This one was new this last June and used at the battle to save Richmond. Our first balloon was kind of a large cotton bag used at the First Battle of Manassas."

"I was there, and I didn't see it!" Gideon declared.

Shrugging, Hunter said, "Maybe it wasn't deployed at the time. Anyway, that first one was heated by pine knots and turpentine, which made lots of hot air. That went up into the open end of the balloon to fill it and make it rise. But the air cooled too fast."

"I don't understand," Gideon said.

Hunter explained, "That meant it couldn't rise very high and it came down quickly as it cooled. It was useful in helping defeat the Yankees. They also have aerial observation balloons. They were used a lot last June and July when the Federals were within a few miles of Richmond. Still, most soldiers have never seen one."

Gideon said, "I wonder if Zeb ever did?"

Hunter turned around. "Why don't we ask him?"

"Yes! It would be something different to talk to him about," Gideon commented, starting back with the correspondent. "It sure got me all excited."

Just then Gideon glanced up ahead and stopped dead still. "Our horses! They're gone!"

A WALL OF SILENCE

It was late afternoon before Gideon returned to Chimborazo and excitedly told Zeb about the stolen horses. Hunter had rented another in order to be back at his military camp before he became absent without leave. Gideon couldn't go because he wasn't experienced enough to ride fast over distance.

Gideon concluded, "I wish you had been with me." He paused, but when Zeb remained as remote and silent as ever, Gideon tried again. "Well, if you didn't like my horse story, try to guess what I saw on the river today."

Zeb's vacant stare remained unchanged even when Gideon enthusiastically told about the war balloon. He repeated details of what Hunter had told him about it.

Gideon added, "He told me that there was a balloon at First Manassas where you and I were together, but I never saw it. Did you?"

For a second, Gideon thought he saw a flicker of change in Zeb's eyes, but it was too fast to be sure.

Gideon continued, "Hunter tells me there were both Union and Confederate balloons at the peninsula campaign the end of June and early July. I heard you helped defend Richmond then. Did you see any balloons at that time?"

Gideon paused, again thinking he noticed a slight change in Zeb's eyes. They seemed to be trying to refocus. But after another few seconds of silence, Gideon straightened up. "I guess not," he admitted sadly.

Taking a deep breath, Gideon declared, "Zeb, it's very hard to carry on a conversation this way, even if I am trying to be a big brother to you. I'll come back again sometime when maybe you'll feel more like talking."

Zeb blinked and slowly brought his eyes to where they met Gideon's. "Don't go," he said in a whisper.

"Zeb! Oh, Zeb!" Gideon yelled joyously, promptly bringing some ambulatory patients and volunteer male nurses running around the corner of the building. Gideon didn't really notice them.

Zeb whispered, "Tell me . . . about . . . the balloon."

Throwing his arms around the other boy, Gideon exclaimed, "Thank God, you're back!"

Zeb's mouth worked briefly before the words came in a low, throaty murmur. "I've been . . . in a faraway place."

Gideon shifted his hands to grip both of Zeb's. "I know!" he said, feeling his face start to contort in joyous tears. "But just hang on to me and you won't ever have to go there again!"

★   ★   ★   ★   ★

After dark, instead of returning to the small but neat cabins where the Yateses' former slaves worked for wages as freedmen, Nat accepted a surprise invitation to have a glass of buttermilk with Mr. and Mrs. Yates. The three of them sat at a wooden table in the spacious kitchen.

Mrs. Yates picked up a white ceramic pitcher from the kitchen table and poured buttermilk into three glasses. "We invited you here," she said, "to ask you some questions, if you don't mind."

By now, Nat was used to his benefactress doing most of the talking. Her husband was a taciturn person who was cordial but not very talkative in the field or at church. Nat replied, "I don't mind. Ask your questions."

Mrs. Yates handed him a filled glass. "Have you decided about speaking to some of my women friends about your experiences in bondage?"

"I would rather not, if you don't mind."

He knew that wasn't the answer she wanted, so he wasn't surprised when she didn't seem to hear.

★   ★

She continued, "The audience would all be loyal Confederates—mostly small farmers' wives and mothers and widows of boys
fighting against the Union. None of them owns slaves, although
they believe it's right to do so. I hope your speaking to them may
change some minds. They are nice people, so you needn't be
afraid."

She glanced around and lowered her voice, although there was
nobody in the house except the three of them. "As you know because we helped you escape from Briarstone that first time, Baruch and I are 'conductors' on the Underground Railroad. You may
have guessed that we are also strong abolitionists. Of course, we
don't let any of that be known, but I'm sure some people, like
William, have a suspicion that we're antislavery."

Knowing how strongly his benefactress wanted him to do this
simple thing for them, Nat explained, "I'm not afraid of speaking
to your friends, although I have never talked to any group. I want
to do this for you both, but if I did, eventually William or Cobb
would hear of it. That would infuriate them even more than they
are now, and I've already got enough troubles with them."

"I understand," Mrs. Yates assured him, "but I have watched
you ever since you came to Briarstone. Baruch and I have quietly
asked a lot of questions about you. We feel rather confident about
our opinions so far, but we need more information. Your speaking
to this group would help us decide if we should share our thoughts
about your possible future."

My future? Nat mentally repeated. The fifteen hundred dollars
he wanted to repay them for buying his freedom was an agonizing
mental burden. It seemed even heavier after he recalled hearing
one of the recent visitors to Briarstone tell about a raise just given
to government clerks in Richmond. Their salary had been in-
creased from twelve hundred dollars a year to fifteen hundred. If
Nat could get a part-time job working as a freedman for various
small farmers, the most he could expect was about sixteen dollars
a month. At that rate, he calculated, it would take about eight
years just to repay Mr. and Mrs. Yates.

Nat told them, "My foreseeable future involves finding my two
brothers and repaying you two."

★ ★

"Ah!" Mrs. Yates exclaimed. "That's what we suspected, so we want you to think like a free-born person and look beyond the foreseeable future."

Nat didn't know how to respond to that, so he sipped his buttermilk and waited.

Mrs. Yates said, "We'll leave the invitation open. Now, Nat, we have another question for you. Have you ever heard of Harriet Tubman?"

"I'm sorry, but no."

"How about Frederick Douglass?"

"No."

"Sojourner Truth?"

Nat raised an eyebrow. "Is that a person's name?"

Mrs. Yates chuckled. "Oh yes, indeed. She chose it herself, but her slave name was Isabella. She was freed, like you, and became an abolitionist. Would you like to know more about her and the other two?"

When he nodded, Mrs. Yates continued. "Harriet Tubman must now be in her early forties. She's led many, many slaves to freedom on the Underground Railroad."

Nat's eyes lit up. Knowing what he had gone through just to rescue his mother, sister, and one brother, he would imagine what great courage Harriet Tubman had to help so many slaves reach freedom.

"Sojourner Truth," Mrs. Yates continued, "is a freed slave who travels throughout the North speaking on emancipation and women's rights. And Frederick Douglass is a slave who escaped about twenty-five years ago. Like you, he's the son of a slave mother and a white father. His abolitionist work includes editing a periodical called the *North Star*."

Mrs. Yates fell silent, as if expecting Nat to make some comments.

He said carefully, "They're remarkable people. I'm glad you told me about them. But are you suggesting I might do something like them?"

"Our thoughts about your future go beyond that," she replied, "but we won't impose our will on you."

★ ★

A WALL OF SILENCE

"I appreciate that," Nat said, "but all I want to do is find my remaining two brothers and rejoin the rest of the family in Canada, where we can all live free."

"Nat, I know you've never had any reason to even hope for a future, but that's changed, and your thinking must change, too. Let me ask you this: If the South loses the war, and President Lincoln frees the slaves, who is going to help them readjust? Who will be their leaders?"

A smile touched Nat's lips. "If you're thinking I could be, I have to disagree. I'm no leader."

Mr. Yates surprised Nat by saying, "You could be."

Nat met the man's somber eyes. "You think so?"

Baruch Yates nodded. "I've watched you work, and I've heard what Clara learned about you from many people. Yes, I really think you could be." He turned to his wife. "Clara can explain it far better than I."

She said quickly, "But that's enough for now, Nat. You think about all this and we'll talk again."

Feeling bewildered and yet intrigued, Nat left for the cabin he shared with another freedman. *Freedom*, he told himself, *is not quite what I expected it to be.*

★ ★ ★ ★ ★

The next day, Gideon was exhausted but excited when he approached the narrow four-story building with the sign covering one side: *Richmond Daily Sun and Printing House*. He had been up much of the night laboriously writing and rewriting the stories Zeb had told him about going into battles carrying only a drum. Hunter hadn't been around to evaluate Gideon's composition, but he felt good about it. He had alternately laughed and brushed away tears as he wrote, recalling how Zeb had talked nonstop for many hours. He told of armed men dying horribly all around him, but Zeb only carried a drum. Most of his personal experiences were so gruesome that Gideon shuddered, and he honestly could not write about them. They were too hideous for the *Sun*'s readers. But out of the horrible stories Zeb had told Gideon had come his firm conviction that he could really write, and he should stay on instead of

★ ★
81

going home. At least, he would remain in Richmond as long as possible.

Pushing open the front door, Gideon told himself with some satisfaction, *I hope Mr. Kerr will like it and will pay some good stringing money. I could sure use it.*

Instead of the usual clerk, whom Gideon had learned was Mr. Franks, Max Hassler sat behind the front desk. He surprised Gideon by smiling at him. It was the first time the boy had ever been cordial.

"Hey, Tugwell," Max asked, "you got your first pair of boots yet?"

That was a sore spot for Gideon because every boy looked forward to when his feet stopped growing and it was safe to invest in a pair of boots. But Gideon was so unexpectedly pleased at his reception that he didn't let it bother him like almost everything else Max did.

"Not yet," he replied, gripping the precious pages he'd written.

"Look at mine!" Max bragged, lifting both legs to show long boots extending almost to his knees. "You ever see nicer ones?"

"No," Gideon admitted, looking toward the closed door to the editorial department. "Is Mr. Kerr in?"

"Yes, but he can't be disturbed." Max glanced at the sheaf of papers. "You got a story for him?"

"Something I wrote. I think he'll like it."

Max noisily dropped his booted feet onto the wooden floor. "Maybe he will and maybe he won't," he said, reverting to his normal annoying manner. "Give it to me and I'll pass it on."

Gideon hesitated. "Uh . . . I could come back—"

"Won't do any good!" Max interrupted. "I'll see that he gets it."

Very reluctantly, Gideon handed the story over and left with an uneasy feeling he couldn't explain.

★ ★ ★ ★ ★

Two weeks after moving in with Mrs. Wheeler, Emily's homesickness had become painful. It wasn't just that she was in the Confederacy that fought against the Union she supported. She didn't have any friends her age. She never saw Julie, and Gideon was still in Richmond.

Emily sat at a small desk in her rented second-story bedroom, with a patchwork quilt over her shoulders. The small fireplace gave little heat. The wind moaned through the eaves and periodically blew into the chimney.

She replaced the quill pen in the inkwell while bare branches of an apple tree scratched on her window with ghostly fingers. Holding her letter closer to the coal-oil lamp, Emily read aloud what she had written.

" 'Dear Gideon, I'm glad that you wrote your mother about the job and finding your friend Zeb. She told me that the surgeons say he is recovering but it will be a long time before he can leave the hospital.

" 'I'm pleased that you finally got down to meet your newspaperman's friend Dunkerton. I'm glad you like him and that you've been able to make your courier trips safely.' "

Satisfied, Emily again picked up her pen.

I read your short letter to me over and over. I know how you must feel about being homesick. Sometimes the feeling almost chokes me; it's that awful. I would love to be home in Illinois with Jessie for Christmas, but I guess that's not to be. Will you get to come home by then?

Emily debated about telling Gideon how his mother had looked Sunday at church. Her eyes were red, as if she had been weeping a lot. When Emily had commented on that to John Fletcher, he told her that he was going to leave the Tugwell farm as soon as someone could be found to replace him. Even though his family was dead and the Yankees had burned his home in the Shenandoah Valley, he wanted to spend Christmas with what few old friends still remained.

"No!" Emily said aloud. "Gideon's seeing his dream come true in Richmond. I won't do anything to hurt that." Instead, she returned to her writing.

Your mother told me that she had written about Nat being

★ ★

sold and then freed by Mr. and Mrs. Yates. I haven't seen him, but Mrs. Yates told me he's working with her husband on their farm. The only fright Nat had was when he heard a pack of hounds baying in the river bottom.

Mr. Yates told me at church that he had protested to Barley Cobb about that. He claimed he was chasing after a raccoon. Mr. Yates told me that's not true. Hounds trained to hunt runaway slaves won't trail any animal. Cobb is doing all he can to scare poor Nat.

I'm in good health and hope you are the same. Write again when you can.

She started to sign her name as a knock sounded at her door.

At Emily's invitation, Mrs. Wheeler entered with a letter. "This just came by private carrier."

Emily quickly stood, took the envelope, and glanced at the return address. "It's from Mrs. Lydia Stonum, a nice lady I stayed with in Richmond some months ago. But why would she send me ... Gideon!" she whispered in sudden alarm. "Maybe something happened to—"

"Don't guess, Emily!" Mrs. Wheeler interrupted kindly but firmly. "Open it!"

With fingers that suddenly trembled, Emily obeyed. She unfolded the letter, which held a second folded sheet. She skimmed the few lines on the first page.

My Dear Emily. I hope you find the enclosed helpful. I'm sorry I can't be your chaperon.

Puzzled, Emily unfolded the second sheet and sucked in her breath at the official-looking letterhead.

"Bad news?" Mrs. Wheeler asked anxiously.

Emily handed over the second sheet, saying in a whisper, "Please—read it aloud."

Mrs. Wheeler cleared her throat. " 'Please permit the bearer to pass at will throughout my command. Signed, Jefferson Davis, President.' "

Mrs. Wheeler gasped. "Emily! Do you know what this means? You've got your passes for Illinois!"

★ ★

DREAMING OF
CHRISTMAS

After the initial surprise of receiving passes signed by the Confederacy's president, Emily said a heartfelt prayer of gratitude. Then she hastily began making plans to return to Illinois.

She enthusiastically told Mrs. Wheeler, "There's so much to do and so little time! Fortunately, I still have the money I didn't spend when Mrs. Stonum and I tried to leave the Confederacy last August. It's not much, but it'll pay for transportation and buy some food."

The words continued to gush from Emily. "I'll have to leave soon, before bad weather makes travel impossible. But I need to find someone to go with me and I must write my friend Jessie and tell her I'm coming. I have to say good-bye to everyone and write Gideon—"

She broke off her flow of words and frowned. "Where will I find someone to travel with me? Maybe Mrs. Yates?"

Her landlady admitted, "She would be a good choice."

"I'll ask her," Emily declared, whirling around the room, her face radiant. "I'm going home! Thank God, I'm going home and in time for Christmas!"

Mrs. Wheeler said, "You mentioned writing your girl friend in Illinois, but remember that there is no regular postal service between the Confederacy and the Union."

Emily groaned. "I forgot that! Well, she and her mother won't mind if I just show up."

"I hope so," Mrs. Wheeler replied. "Now, what if Clara Yates can't go with you? What'll you do then?"

"I don't know, but I'll find somebody."

Sighing, Mrs. Wheeler said, "I would love to see my sister in Chicago. She and I are the last of our family."

Emily stopped dead still. "Oh, Mrs. Wheeler! I forgot all about that! Would you like to be my chaperon?"

Smiling, she replied, "When can we leave?"

★　★　★　★　★

Nat was drawn to the secret slave church services held Sunday nights deep in the woods. Slaves had been prohibited from preaching since a black preacher, Nat Turner, led a bloody revolt thirty-one years before. Many white folks fervently believed that Turner had been demented, but to some of those in bondage, Turner had done what they often thought about but didn't dare act out.

Many slaves preferred their own form of religious expression instead of being confined to the balcony or back of the white folks' churches. Those services tended to be formal and rigid, with little opportunity to joyously celebrate the hope and joy that was the message from the black pulpit.

In the clandestine "hush-arbor" meetings, the exuberant singing and hand-clapping afforded relief from dawn-to-dusk labor. Their exhorter, Brother Tynes, was a master at stirring his audiences. Even Nat had been influenced by Tynes' quoting of Scripture and then applying it in a practical way to his fellow bondsmen's lives.

Nat had a more compelling, personal reason for attending Brother Tynes' sermon. Delia probably would be there. So Nat deliberately arrived early, slipping through the evening darkness, glad that there was no snow to leave telltale tracks. Then he chided himself. *I'm free! I don't have to worry about William or Cobb as long as I keep away from them!*

By the flickering light of the two pine torches flanking the crude altar, Nat saw that the little preacher with the big voice hadn't yet arrived. However, a rather heavyset woman had already stuck her head inside the great iron pot. She shouted in religious fervor, her voice muffled so that it didn't travel far. Nat stayed near the end of the little clearing, closer to the thick sheltering trees.

★　★

A bright smile lit up his face as Delia slipped out of the woods and into the pale light of the torches.

"You came back!" she exclaimed, returning his smile.

"It was worth the risk," he said softly.

She understood his meaning and demurely dropped her eyes. "I heard that you were freed, Nat. When you didn't come these past weeks, I thought you stayed away because you were afraid one of us would tell William."

"I certainly thought about it," Nat admitted, resisting an urge to touch her hands. "If William knew I came here, he could have Barley Cobb waiting for me with his hounds. I don't want to lose my freedom again."

"No one who comes here would betray you," Delia assured him, looking tenderly at him. "That would cause William and all the other masters in the area to not only stop our services, but everyone would be whipped for leaving the plantations without permission."

"That's why I finally decided to come," Nat said. "That and . . ." He stopped, unable to express the feelings he had for her. He was free, but she was still a slave and had no choice about her future. He suggested, "We'd better sit down."

Delia seemed disappointed, but she started walking with him toward the split logs that served as benches.

A voice from behind called, "Delia! Wait!"

She and Nat turned together to see a tall, slender youth hurrying out of the woods toward them.

Nat lowered his voice. "Who's that?"

"Name's Caesar," Delia whispered. "Young Master William bought him to replace you. I don't like him."

"Why not?"

"He asks too many questions. I think he's spying on all of us."

Delia didn't offer to introduce him to Nat, and he didn't care because Caesar promptly joined them without being asked. He sat down on the cold benches, sandwiching Delia between him and Nat. As the benches slowly filled, Caesar talked to Delia about events in the manor while ignoring Nat.

Nat was relieved as the singing started, forcing an end to

★　★

Caesar's chatter. Delia joined in the spirited singing, occasionally giving Nat a sly smile. Nat twice noticed Caesar glowering at him over Delia's head.

Following the singing and prayers, Brother Tynes mounted the stump after the log benches were all filled. The light from the two pine torches reflected off of his face. He was short; not over five feet tall, with a smooth, dark face and curly gray hair. But there was nothing little about his voice. It was deep and rich and quickly swept his audience up with power and conviction.

He had no Bible because it was illegal for a slave to read. He wasn't officially a preacher because, after Turner's revolt, laws prohibited slaves from preaching. Tynes called himself an exhorter and quoted the Scripture verses he had heard in his white master's church.

"Of all de people in dis heah land," he began quietly, "ain't many got mo' temptation dan us to hate dem what keeps us in chains."

There was a murmur of agreement before he continued. His voice rose slightly.

"Dey done sol' my mammy away from me whilst I was still too little to carry water to de field han's. When I was growed, dey done chose a wife fo' me. We had fo' fine chilluns—" His voice cracked, and he paused.

Nat glanced at Delia in the dark and saw her dabbing at her eyes. Nat quickly turned away so he wouldn't embarrass her.

When Tynes continued, his voice was thick with emotion. "We loved dem chilluns borned to her an' me. She cried long and powerful hard when dey was snatched away. We never seed dem again—never!"

Brother Tynes' voice rose until it echoed back from the surrounding woods. "Muh heart like to break same as muh woman's, but de massa, he don' lak fo' to see no slave wid a sad face, no suh!"

From the audience, someone said aloud, "Dat's de troof, bruddah!"

Tynes went on, "Ol' massa, he lay de bullwhip on muh back fo' no reason 'cept I hurt deep down inside where ain't no grease can ease de pain. Muh woman, she know bettah dan to try to stop de whip, but she done it. De massa, he turn on her wid it. She—" His voice broke again, and he dropped his head.

Regaining his composure, the exhorter said softly, "Nex' mawnin', she daid."

A single, collective gasp came from the congregation. Nat gulped, recalling hearing about a white mistress who had whipped a woman slave to death. Nat had no doubt Tynes spoke the truth about his wife.

"Ah knows," Tynes said, "y'all done felt de same pain as me, some maybe mo' dan me. But we all been treated like de massa's chickens and pigs: all white man's prop'ty to do wid as he wants. Ain't no way to change dat. From de moment we borned till we dies, we's slaves.

"So's we got reason to hate," he added. "We got mo' reason dan most fo'ks; we sho' do. But de Good Book done say we gots to love 'stead o' hatin'!"

Up to those last few words, Nat had found himself nodding in agreement. But his head abruptly changed to shaking from side to side, silently rejecting the thought.

When Tynes spoke again, his voice was so low that Nat and the others had to lean forward to hear better.

"Yassuh, we sho' got reason to hate, but we don'. We don' hit back when da massa whip us. Why? 'Cause de Good Book done say dis, 'What y'all want done to yo'se'ves, ye do de same to dem!' "

Nat felt Delia lean toward him. She whispered, "I heard my last massa say that's called the Golden Rule."

Nodding, Nat's mind instantly filled with names of people he could easily hate. William Lodge. Barley Cobb. Nat emotionally resisted the thought that he could treat those two the way he would like to be treated.

Nat's mind drifted away, twisting and tumbling as he struggled with the concept of that rule. He retreated deep into his own reflections, struggling mightily with the warring factions within.

I wonder, he thought to himself, *if I could follow that teaching if the opportunity came?*

Nat's musings switched to Mrs. Yates's invitation to speak to the group of women. *If I did talk to Mrs. Yates's friends, I'd like to speak with power like Brother Tynes. But I'm not going to address them. I don't want to stir up William and Cobb and make them any more determined to sell me back into slavery than they already are!*

Nat turned his head to look at Delia and saw that Caesar was also looking at her. Nat's and Caesar's eyes met and locked. There was something in Caesar's face that made Nat refuse to look away first. The silent clash continued for several seconds before Caesar blinked. Nat turned back to watch the preacher but decided he agreed with Delia; he didn't like Caesar, either.

★　★　★　★　★

Two weeks after reluctantly handing his first story to Max Hassler, Gideon headed for the *Sun*. Knowing how short-tempered the editor was, Gideon planned to first hand him a new story he'd written about Hannah Chandler's highly dangerous job in a munitions factory. Then Gideon would politely ask when his story would run about Zeb's experiences as a drummer boy in combat. It wasn't just that Gideon wanted to see his work in print; he needed the money.

A ragged newsboy stood on the corner outside the *Sun* building, shouting, "Read all about it! Drummer boy helps save Richmond!"

That sounds like Zeb's story! The thought excited Gideon. He fished in his pocket for two cents. After exchanging the precious cents for the paper, Gideon skimmed the printed story. A few minor changes had been made, but there was no doubt that most of it was exactly as Gideon had written it. He let out a joyous yell and rushed toward the newspaper's door.

★　★　★　★　★

Happily entering the *Sun*'s front office, Gideon was disappointed that Max Hassler was again behind the front desk instead of Mr. Franks. But Gideon was so happy, he exclaimed, "I'm a published writer! This is my story!" He excitedly tapped the page. "Right here!"

★　★

Max asked indifferently, "What makes you think it's your story? Does it have your name on it?"

"You know there are no names on stories, but this is mine! I handed it to you a couple of weeks ago."

"You're wrong, Tugwell! I wrote that story."

Gideon dropped the newspaper on the counter and stared in disbelief. "What?"

"You heard me. I wrote that story. Ask old man Kerr. He'll tell you. He even said it wasn't bad."

It took a moment for the awful realization to sink into Gideon's heart. "You've got to tell him the truth!"

Abruptly standing, Max glowered across the counter. "You want to make trouble, Tugwell? I'll give it to you if you don't get out of here right now! But first, I'll take that." He yanked Gideon's new story from his hands.

"Give that back!" Gideon exclaimed. "Give it back so I can turn it in to Mr. Kerr myself!"

"No, Tugwell. You're not going to see the old cuss, and besides, it's my story. Now, do you want to leave quietly, or shall I call old man Kerr and let you try to convince him that a redneck cracker could actually write anything publishable?"

For a long moment, Gideon was so shocked he couldn't think straight. *It's my word against his, and I have no proof!* he told himself. *I'd better calm down before I decide what to do.* He turned and hurried out of the building, followed by Max's mocking laughter.

★　★　★　★　★

Gideon's gloom over having his work stolen by Max was somewhat lessened by Zeb's rapid recovery. Three weeks after Gideon had first seen Zeb at the hospital, healing of both his mind and body even surprised the surgeons. Mrs. Stonum told Gideon that they credited this to Zeb's youthful constitution and having found a real, caring friend around his own age. The next time Gideon visited, Zeb was carefully using his good arm to help some of the others help those whose wounds were more serious.

"Big news, Gideon!" he called. "The surgeon says I can leave the hospital for short periods, so I'd like to go with you the next time you pick up a story from Herb Hunter."

Gideon quickly decided not to mention his own problem, which could spoil his friend's glad report. "That's great, Zeb! I'll be glad to have you along!"

"Can you get me a ride on a wagon or something?" Zeb asked. "I probably can't ride a horse that far, and I sure can't walk all that way."

"We'll find something," Gideon assured him. "I'm sure pleased that you're your old self again."

Zeb glanced around and dropped his voice so the other patients couldn't hear him. "I heard the surgeon tell your friend Mrs. Stonum that if I had a family, I could even go home to finish recovering."

A tinge of homesickness swept over Gideon. He was grateful that he wasn't an orphan like Emily, Hannah, and Zeb. But as Christmas neared, a longing to be home, even for a few days, grew inside him.

"Well, Zeb," he said, trying to sound cheerful, "since I'm now your big brother, and I can't get home to my family, it's nice that we have each other."

Zeb asked, "Aren't you going home for Christmas?"

Home for Christmas after being away on my own the first time, Gideon thought.

Nostalgia engulfed Gideon so quickly that he had to fight to keep from showing how deeply affected he was. "No," he finally answered Zeb. "I don't think I'll make it this year."

"Oh." Zeb's response was loaded with disappointment.

Gideon was touched. He declared, "But if I did, maybe you could come with me."

"Could I?" Zeb's voice lifted in hope.

"Yes, of course, but as I told you . . ." He paused as Mrs. Stonum hurried toward them.

"I thought I'd find you two together," she said with a warm smile. "Gideon, I was just leaving the house when a private carrier brought this letter for you."

Startled, he glanced at the envelope and recognized Emily's

handwriting. He hurriedly opened it and skimmed the few words before a low moan escaped his lips.

"Bad news?" Mrs. Stonum anxiously asked.

Gideon shook his head. "No. Emily got the passes you sent, so she's going back to Illinois."

"That sounds good, so why did you groan?" Zeb asked.

"I didn't realize I did," Gideon answered quietly. "I'm very glad for her, and I thank you, Mrs. Stonum, for making that possible for her."

"You're welcome, Gideon." She turned to Zeb. "I think Gideon is glad for Emily but sorry he won't get to see her when he goes back home."

It's more than that, Gideon realized with great pain. *I may never see her again!*

★　★　★　★　★

In spite of the danger that Barley Cobb might try to kidnap him if Nat left the Yateses' farm, he decided to risk looking for his brother Amos. With papers showing his manumitted status, in case patrollers stopped him, Nat threw an old saddle on a borrowed plow horse and rode toward a nearby small farm. He had heard that the owner, named Stokes, kept only one slave boy. Nat believed this might be Amos.

The farmer was repairing a snake fence when Nat reined in beside him and politely removed his hat. "Mr. Stokes?"

The old man looked up with watery eyes. "Yes."

Nat dropped the slave dialect he used in front of white people to help augment his status as a freedman.

"Mr. Baruch Yates suggested you might have some work for an extra hand. I'm a freedman with papers, and I'm willing to work hard at any jobs you might have."

The farmer cocked his head. "Are you called Nat?"

Surprised, he nodded. "Yes, sir."

"Can't help you," Stokes replied curtly.

Stung at the rebuke but still determined to learn what he had come for, Nat said, "I understand you have only one slave, a boy named Amos."

★　★

"Did have. Sold him."

Nat's heart plummeted in his chest. "Oh? When?"

"Not that it's any of your business," the farmer replied sharply, scowling up at the youth on horseback, "but he's been gone two weeks, maybe three."

Nat asked, "May I ask who bought him?"

"Don't know. Sold at auction. Why're you so interested, boy?"

Nat swallowed hard at the slur, but kept his voice calm. "I think he might be my brother."

"Don't know about that. Now, I got work to do."

Nat paused, then asked, "How did you know my name?"

"William Lodge told every white man around how you stole from him. No decent man would hire you to even shovel manure. Now, ride on, boy."

Crushed at the double news of his brother's sale and William's vindictive campaign to keep him from hiring out, Nat turned the horse back down the lane.

LOOKING BEYOND
THE WAR

On Thursday night, with Hunter back in camp, Gideon visited with Mrs. Stonum and Hannah in their home. He didn't want to be alone with his thoughts about what to do over Max stealing his stories.

Gideon sat in the widow's parlor, facing her and Hannah. She said, "I've been reading the stories you wrote about me and Zeb. I think you're a fine writer. You'll be famous someday."

Gideon was unsettled by her unexpected praise. "Thanks," he murmured.

Hannah asked, "In a bayonet charge, is it true that soldiers lower their heads like they would in a heavy rain and blindly run toward the enemy?"

Gideon nodded. "That's what Zeb told me."

Hannah mused, "I wonder why? Is it because they don't really want to see what terrible thing they're about to do with their bayonets?"

"Zeb didn't tell me that, and I didn't ask."

Mrs. Stonum said, "I find it hard to believe that Zeb has seen our gallant boys trading tobacco and other items with the Union enemy troops across little streams."

"It's true," Gideon assured her. "As Zeb said in the story, the soldiers exchange items by putting them on a little board and pulling it across by strings."

"But the next day," Mrs. Stonum said, "Zeb claims those same soldiers often battled each other. How can people with the same language and the same God peacefully trade one minute and kill each other the next?"

"I don't know," Gideon admitted. "But as Zeb said, the officers don't like it."

"War is so terrible!" the widow said softly.

Gideon guided the conversation to his second published story. "Hannah, did I get everything right about your work in the ordinance laboratory?"

"Oh yes. It was nice of you to name some of the workers besides me, and to say that the youngest girl is just nine and the oldest woman is sixty-seven. Widows and orphans, mostly. Of course, a few boys and men work there. It's good for them to get a little recognition for our part in winning this war for the Confederacy."

Gideon hesitantly said, "Hannah, I don't want to scare you, but I'm concerned about all that powder floating in the air and the room being heated by a coal-burning stove. If one of those primers went off—"

"We have no choice!" she interrupted. "There are seventy of us workers, and this is about the only work we can get. For us, a dollar and a half for a twelve-hour day is good money."

An ominous silence settled over the room. Gideon thought it might help to talk about his troubles with Max, but he decided against it. He left early.

★ ★ ★ ★ ★

Emily had no idea how tediously long, difficult, and frustrating her trip north would be with Mrs. Wheeler. Railcars had been diverted to military use. Horse-drawn commercial vehicles didn't keep regular schedules, so the two travelers took a series of hacks out of Church Creek. For a while, sentinels stopped them about every fifteen miles. However, President Jefferson Davis's passes quickly opened the way all through Confederate lines. By the time they were nearing the Union lines, a strong bond had developed between the travelers.

Sighing, Mrs. Wheeler wistfully said, "I wish you could go on to Chicago with me. You're such a big help and so patient with my handicap. I know my sister would welcome you, and she has a big house."

"Thank you, Mrs. Wheeler, but I don't ever plan to leave Hickory Grove once we get there."

"I understand how you feel, Emily, but I'll talk to my sister. Please give me your address so I can write you after I hear what she says."

Emily fondly smiled at her companion. "I'll give you Jessie's address, but please don't get your hopes up."

As Emily and Mrs. Wheeler crossed into the North, they were immediately challenged by a Federal cavalry troop. Their young lieutenant boldly swept Emily with his eyes before grinning appreciatively. "Well, now, what have we here? I do believe it's a pretty secesh gal and her mama. How'd you two get into our lines?"

Emily quickly bristled. "I'm not a secessionist! And she is not my mother. Mrs. Wheeler's husband was against the South seceding, and we're going home to friends and relatives in Illinois."

The lieutenant admitted, "You don't sound like a Rebel. But you didn't answer my question: How did you get through to our lines?"

"With these." Emily pulled a pass from her reticule.

The officer quickly scanned the pass, then shook his head. "Ol' Jeff Davis doesn't impress us Yankees. You'll both have to come with us."

"Why?" Emily questioned in sudden alarm. "The weather's getting worse and we've got to get to Illinois before the roads are impassible!"

"That's right," Mrs. Wheeler said, lifting her cane to show gnarled fingers. "And this weather is making my bones ache something awful. I promise you that neither of us will say or do anything against the Union, now or later."

"Sorry, ladies," the lieutenant replied. "We'll give you both a cavalry escort to see the major."

Sighing, Emily remembered how the Confederate military had forced her and Mrs. Stonum to turn back on the first attempt to reach Illinois. Now she anguished about these Union troops. *Will we ever get to Illinois?*

★ ★

★ ★ ★ ★ ★

The morning was clear in Richmond when Zeb's surgeon permitted the boy to leave the hospital for a courier trip with Gideon. They caught a ride with a slave driving a heavy wagon headed for Fredericksburg. That's where Gideon was to pick up a story from Hunter. To avoid trouble with authorities, the driver required the boys to stay out of sight under the wagon's canvas cover.

In answer to Gideon's questions, the driver explained that he got no pay but the military paid his master sixteen dollars a month to drive supplies between Richmond and Fredericksburg. When the conversation died down, Gideon pulled the canvas flap back to peer out to see how much farther they had to travel. He blinked, then called to Zeb, "Look!"

The other boy eased up beside Gideon and exclaimed, "A war balloon! But it's not the bright and shiny one I saw at the battle outside of Richmond."

Their driver said from his outside seat, "Dat one not belong to de so'jers. Dis one own by a white man."

Zeb mused, "I heard some men made their own balloons before the war." He snapped his fingers and his face lit up. "Gideon, let's get out and go look at it up close."

Gideon was reluctant. "Mr. Dunkerton should be waiting for me to pick up Herb Hunter's story."

"Ah, you don't have to be in a hurry!" Zeb scoffed. He pushed the canvas flap open. "Come on! We can look at the balloon, then walk from here to that farmer's place."

After a moment's hesitation, Gideon thanked the driver, then scrambled over the tailgate after Zeb. Gideon had an uneasy feeling as they hurried toward the huge balloon tethered in a grove of trees.

★ ★ ★ ★ ★

At Baruch Yates's insistence, Nat always worked the farm within sight of Mr. Yates or the other freedmen. Nat appreciated their concern and tried to be encouraged that he might still find his brother Amos. But along with that hope, Nat silently dealt with the fear that Cobb would try to catch him and resell him back into slavery.

This was in the back of Nat's mind when, for the fourth straight day, he and Mr. Yates drove the heavy sledge to the river bottom at the back end of the farm. One of the countless trees growing there had fallen, crashing through a split-rail fence through which three hogs had escaped. Two had been recaptured, but a third was still on the loose.

When the sledge was loaded with sawed limbs, the older man said, "My wife asked me this morning if you'd said anything to indicate you'd changed your mind about telling her women friends about life as a slave."

"No, I haven't."

"Too bad. Clara and I both think such an experience would open your eyes to some freedom possibilities that you apparently haven't even dreamed about."

"Now that I'm free, my dream is still to find my two missing brothers and help them escape to Canada."

"I understand that. But have you seriously thought about your future when this war is over?"

"That depends on whether the North or the South wins. If the South does, I'll probably be forced back into slavery."

"But if the Union wins," Mr. Yates observed, "and Lincoln's Emancipation Proclamation goes into effect, four million slaves, mostly uneducated and unskilled, are going to be free. They'll be worse off than a flock of sheep with no shepherd. They will need someone like you to lead them out of the dark days they'll face in their newfound freedom."

A smile touched Nat's lips. "I'm no leader, Mr. Yates. I was born a slave, and every day of my life until recently, I've had a master who told me what to do and even what to think."

"You're selling yourself short, Nat. You are one of the very few literate black people in the Confederacy. You're intelligent and have great courage. After all, you twice escaped from Briarstone, and each time you found part of your family and sent them to safety in Canada."

Mr. Yates added, "Those are leadership qualities, Nat. So while

★ ★

you may not be a Harriet Tubman, you should be preparing for whatever the future holds for you and all who are now in bondage."

Nat raised an eyebrow. This was one of the longest comments his usually taciturn benefactor had ever said. "You really think so?"

"I know so, as does my wife." Mr. Yates picked up the reins and stepped up on the front of the sledge. "Tell you what, Nat, I'll drive this load up to the house and have one of the other men help me unload it. Would you mind staying here and fixing the fence so the stock won't get out?"

Nat replied, "You go ahead."

"Good. I'll only be a few minutes. When I get back, we'll try to find that missing hog," the farmer replied and clucked to the team. The sledge moved away.

Nat welcomed the silence of the farm as he dragged the broken fence rails aside to replace them with new ones. Slipping a new rail into place, Nat thought, *I can't imagine what they think I could possibly do after the war. But after I've found the rest of my family so we're all reunited, and I've paid off the money paid for my freedom, what then? Do I stay here?*

Nat suddenly realized the river bottom's heavy undergrowth and dense stands of trees was a good place for a slave catcher to capture Nat alone. His eyes probed the brush and trees, then swept on to take in the farmhouse and outbuildings a half mile away. Relieved at the quiet, pastoral scene, Nat again bent to his work.

Maybe, he told himself, *I should change my mind and talk to those women. It seems that only then will I find out what the Yateses think I might do in—*

His thoughts snapped off at the squealing sound from some brush near the river. He muttered, "That's got to be the missing hog. He sounds hurt."

Nat hesitated, again searching the area, but saw no signs of Cobb. Satisfied, Nat ran toward the hog's cries.

★　★　★　★　★

In openmouthed amazement, Gideon and Zeb walked by a strange six-wheeled wagon with two long extensions running toward the gray balloon. It was tied among the trees, out of Union troops' sight. A weblike covering of countless interlocking strands circled the top of the balloon and converged just above the basket resting upright on the ground.

A short man in his fifties and wearing civilian clothes stepped out of a grove of trees and met the boys. He asked, "Isn't she a beauty?"

Gideon said, "I never saw one so big before."

"I did," Zeb declared. "At the battle for Richmond. It looked like it was made of ladies' silk dresses. But I never seen one up close."

Extending his hand and grinning, the man said, "I'm Lloyd Chapman, aeronaut. I made this balloon myself, same as I did one I flew before the war."

Gideon introduced himself and Zeb, saying, "May we look at it up close, Mr. Chapman?"

"Yes, of course. You can even get in the basket, but be careful of that mooring line. I just filled the bag with gas from that field gas generator." He pointed to the strange six-wheeled wagon with the hoses extending from the rear. He continued, "Our boys captured it from the Yankees. The South doesn't have any more balloons, so they let me see if I could fill this one so they can get up a couple hundred feet in the air and see what the enemy is doing. I'm about ready to let them do that."

Zeb hoisted himself over the high-sided basket and exclaimed, "Look at me, Gideon! I'm a balloon man!"

"Balloonist," Chapman corrected him good-naturedly as Gideon joined his young friend. "But those of us who experimented with balloons before the war like to call ourselves aeronauts or airmen."

Gideon gazed up at the monstrous bag overhead. "How high up in the air can this thing go?"

"Well," Mr. Chapman explained, "with the gas instead of hot air, which I used to use, maybe three hundred feet. You see, our observers have to get up out of range of Yankee guns. I was at Richmond during the Peninsula Campaign and saw that the Yankees started shooting small arms as soon as our balloon rose above the treetops. They even used cannons until—Wait! Don't touch that!"

Gideon spun around at the sharp command just as Zeb jerked his hands back from a rope. "I'm sorry, mister!"

The balloon suddenly lurched upward. The owner made a frantic grab for the basket to hold it down, but it was too late.

"Noooo!" Zeb screeched as the balloon rose so rapidly, the man had to drop off. The loss of his weight caused the balloon to spurt skyward with both boys shrieking in sudden terror.

★ ★

A WILD
BALLOON RIDE

Nat pushed through the brambles, his eyes probing ahead, trying to locate the squealing hog. He was not concerned about Cobb because there had been no baying of his vicious hounds, so Nat's mind was free to continue his thoughts about talking to Mrs. Yates's friends.

I should ask her more about Frederick Douglass, Sojourner Truth, and Harriet Tubman, he decided. *What do they say when they speak to white audiences? And what should I say to those women that won't offend them yet will still tell the truth about my life as a slave?*

Through the underbrush, close to the river, which Nat could now smell, he glimpsed a reddish-colored hog wildly thrashing about and squealing loudly. Nat had expected to find the animal stuck under a log or caught between a couple of low tree trunks. That didn't seem to be the case, because the hog's body whipped back and forth, yet his head couldn't come up. He shook it vigorously but vainly.

Nat pushed the last bush aside and got his first clear view of the animal. *That's our runaway, but how did he get a rope around his neck?*

"Don't move!" Cobb's harsh voice commanded from behind.

Nat froze in position but turned his head enough to see the slave catcher step from behind a tree. He held a double-barreled shotgun in his hands.

"Ye ain't got enough smarts to git away from me," he said with

★ ★
103

a satisfied chuckle. "Now, ye jist hold right still whilst I slip these here hand irons on ye."

Nat helplessly watched Cobb shift the weapon to his left hand. With the other, he reached into his right jacket pocket and produced a pair of iron cuffs. The short chain between them clanked as he stepped forward.

★　★　★　★　★

Emily and Mrs. Wheeler were interrogated in a small cabin by a Major Daniel Bonham, a stocky, balding officer wearing a dark blue jacket and pale blue trousers. It wasn't easy for Emily to be patient, knowing that she was finally inside Union lines, yet she and her chaperon could still be sent back to the Confederacy. *Oh, Lord!* Emily silently prayed. *Don't let them stop us now.*

The major said to Mrs. Wheeler, "So you're a widow going to Chicago to visit your only living sister?" When Mrs. Wheeler nodded, he turned to Emily. "And you're an orphan heading to Illinois to stay with your childhood friend Jessie Barlow and her mother?"

"Yes, in Hickory Grove," Emily replied. "When my brothers and parents died before the war started, Mrs. Barlow invited me to come live with them. But I had to go live with my only other relatives, Uncle Silas Lodge and his family in Virginia. I've wanted to return to Illinois for a long time but couldn't."

"How come you know Jeff Davis?" the major asked suspiciously.

"I don't know him," Emily explained. "A woman who befriended me knows him, and she got the passes for me."

"Are you planning on returning to the Confederacy?" Bonham inquired.

"No, sir. Once I get back home, I never expect to leave again."

"What if you marry after the war and your husband wants to live in the South?"

"I haven't thought much about getting married."

"Do you have a beau, miss?"

Emily didn't see how that was any of the major's business, but she didn't want to annoy him. "No, sir."

"Not even any of those Rebel boys in Virginia?"

★　★

Emily thought of Gideon but told herself, *We're just friends*. "No, sir," she answered.

Bonham replied, "I'm just trying to determine if you have some strong emotional ties to the Confederacy that might make you change your mind, maybe betray the Union."

"Sir, I resent that!" Emily snapped and instantly regretted it. *Don't make him angry!* she warned herself.

He replied, "Don't get upset! I'm just doing my duty to determine if either of you are Rebel sympathizers."

Mrs. Wheeler declared, "We're not! Many years ago I married a Southerner, a small farmer. In the referendum right after the war started, he voted against secession."

"Then he was in the minority," the officer answered. "For every one like your husband, two voted to secede. I assume he wasn't a slaveholder?"

"We didn't believe in slavery," the widow explained.

"I certainly don't, either!" Emily emphatically declared. "I always defended President Lincoln during my stay in the South, and that often got me into trouble."

The major smiled. "You seem like a saucy one, miss."

"I just try to do what's right."

Major Bonham's smile slowly widened to a grin. "I believe you, miss."

Sensing that the officer's attitude was softening, she replied respectfully, "Thank you, sir."

Mrs. Wheeler volunteered, "A woman friend of mine and I both think Emily should become a teacher and return to the South after the war. Slaves should be free by then, and their children will need teachers."

Emily caught a glint of suspicion in the major's eyes, so she quickly declared, "As I said, I don't ever plan on leaving Illinois."

The abrupt look of misgiving faded from Bonham's eyes. "I believe that, too. Now, back to the business at hand. You said the Barlows have a son in the Union cavalry who had been wounded. How old is he?"

"Nineteen or twenty. His mother said I could have Brice's room while he's gone."

★ ★

"Do you write him, miss?"

She sensed the officer was now teasing her. She dropped her eyes. "He asked me to, but you know how hard it is for letters to get through these days."

"Did he ever ask for a lock of your hair?"

It was a very common request by soldiers, who wore the precious strands next to their hearts. "Yes." Emily felt a flush in her cheeks because Brice had repeatedly said that he was going to marry her when she grew up.

The major was obviously teasing her when he slyly asked, "Are you going to see him?"

"It's not likely, with him being away in the war."

"I suppose you're right." The officer quickly wrote something before rising and facing Mrs. Wheeler. "These are your papers," he said. "You shouldn't have any more trouble the rest of the way. Welcome back to the Union and have a safe trip home!"

★　★　★　★　★

The immense balloon drifted above the treetops before Gideon and Zeb stopped shrieking. They clutched the high sides of the wicker basket in which they stood. Their hope of being stopped from a wild ride faded as the balloon's owner failed to catch the dangling end of the rope, which Zeb had unintentionally released.

Zeb gave a nervous laugh. "I always wanted to go up in one of these things!" he declared. "Look out there! You can see forever in all directions."

Gideon tore his eyes away from the ground and the trees that silently slid away below him. His fears eased as he shifted his gaze to a panorama of wondrous sights. "Sure can!" he agreed.

Zeb said, "Look at all the people staring up at us. I bet they ain't never seen such a sight!"

Gideon looked down and realized they were almost all women and children with only a few older men. All the young men were off fighting the Yankees.

Zeb pointed down. "Almost below us is Marye's Heights, and past that, closer to town, there's the sunken road and a stone wall. See them?"

"Yes, but how do you know that's what we're seeing?"

"When there was no fighting, sometimes things got so boring that I watched one of the officers drawing maps. He even learned me to read some words on the maps."

Gideon nodded as Zeb pointed out the Rappahannock River, with a large boat tied up to the shore. Zeb identified two church steeples, the plank road, the railroad tracks, and in the country- side, a few scattered farmhouses in open fields.

Zeb explained, "When we whupped the Yankees at the Second Battle of Manassas at the end of August, bluecoats also evacuated Fredericksburg. But my friend who draws maps believes the Yan- kees will have to retake it in order to attack Richmond again. So let's keep a sharp eye out for . . . Look!"

Alarmed by the sudden urgency in Zeb's voice, Gideon followed his friend's outstretched arm. Beyond the river, a long blue ribbon moved along the countryside like a string of ants. Gideon asked, "What's that?"

"Yankees!" Zeb whispered. "We're drifting straight toward them, and they've got a cannon!"

"You sure?"

"Positive! See those teams of horses? They're pulling a can- non!" Zeb looked straight up at the huge mass of balloon over- head. "We've got to turn this around!"

"I don't think it can be steered." Gideon's voice rose with ten- sion. "It goes where the wind blows!" The balloon was nearly across the river as he started to again glance toward the advancing troops. Out of the corner of his eye, he caught a puff of smoke just beyond the riverbank's far side. "What's that, Zeb?"

"Yankees! Get down!" he shouted, grabbing Gideon's arm and falling with him in the basket's small, confined space just as a ball snarled harmlessly by. It was followed by a second that sounded like an angry hornet before it struck one of the balloon's many strands. A moment later, the sound of two fired muskets reached them.

"What do we do?" Gideon asked from where he crouched low.

"Stay down and pray! I only saw two Yankees, but there may

be more of them, and they could have a cannon hidden down there with them!"

★ ★ ★ ★ ★

Nat fought down a panicked feeling as Cobb eased up behind him with the shotgun in his left hand and the handirons in the other. *Think!* Nat told himself. *Mama always said that winning is in the mind and not the muscles, so think fast!*

"Hold still!" the slave catcher ordered. "Put your hands behind your back, real slow-like."

Nat cast a longing eye toward the Yateses' farmhouse in hopes of seeing Mr. Yates returning, but there was no sign of him. Nat realized that if he was to escape, it had to be before his wrists were secured. Frantically, he glanced around, looking for anything that might help him avoid being resold into slavery.

The roped hog made choking sounds and stopped thrashing about. He leaned so far back that his hindquarters almost touched the ground. It was a desperate effort to break the rope or pull it over his thick neck. But the harder he pulled, the tighter the noose became. The other end of the rope stretched tautly against the tree trunk where it had been tied.

Nat turned his upper body toward Cobb, asking, "Where're your hounds?"

"To home. They cain't be quiet-like when they smell yore kind." Cobb dropped his eyes to the cuffs. One had become entangled with the short chain attached to the other. Cobb added, "I been a-watchin' ye an' a-waitin' muh chance. When I seen that loose hog here yestiddy, I jist brought me a coupla ears o' corn fer bait and a rope. When that blasted farmer done left ye alone, it were easy as shootin' fish in a rain bar'l to ketch ye."

Nat made his move just as he saw the cuff fall free of the chain. "Yahhhhh!" he yelled with all his might and leaped over the rope. Behind him, Nat heard the cuffs drop and knew that Cobb was shifting the gun into firing position. At the sound of the weapon being cocked, Nat's gooseflesh erupted in fear. But he landed on his feet, bent over, and slapped the hog's rump hard.

Instantly squealing, the animal swung away from him, snag-

★ ★

ging the taut rope on the slave catcher's legs. He staggered backward, trying to keep his balance. The gun tilted upward and both barrels roared.

Nat whirled away and darted into the sheltering trees, his heart pounding—but he was still free.

★ ★ ★ ★ ★

After the two shots were fired at them, Gideon and Zeb crouched low in their airborne basket, heads down, eyes closed in earnest prayer. Two more deadly balls whistled by, followed by a whirling sound approaching at high speed. "What's that?" Gideon asked.

Before Zeb could answer, something whooshed by below them, followed by a heavy booming sound from across the river. "Cannon!" Zeb breathed, his eyes wide with fright. "They missed us, probably because they can't tilt the barrel up far enough. If they hit it, and the gas goes out while we're over this river . . ."

"Don't say it!" Gideon cried, vainly glancing around the basket in hopes of seeing something he could do to make the balloon rise faster or change direction. There was nothing. The balloon was not made for free flight, but was raised and lowered by long ropes held by men on the ground or pulled by horses.

The basket lurched slightly. From where he crouched in the bottom, Gideon asked Zeb, "Did you feel that?"

"Wind's shifted!" Zeb declared. He quickly raised up just enough so that he could see over the basket's high side. "We're blowing back the way we came!"

Gideon started to yell joyfully, but froze at the sight of a grove of trees straight ahead. "We're going down!"

Zeb glanced at the balloon overhead. "I don't think they hit us, so the air overhead must be cooling, making the balloon go down."

The boys exchanged fearful looks, and Gideon knew Zeb was thinking the same thing: *Where? On top of the Yankees or on the Confederate side?*

The uncertainty was too much for Gideon. He raised up just enough to peer over the side. "We're safe!" he exclaimed. "We're almost down to treetop level on our side of the river! We're safe, Zeb! Safe!"

★　★　★　★　★

Days later, Emily turned her gaze from the familiar Illinois prairies, where they had been traveling in a rented hack. She focused on a sturdy two-story farmhouse as the horse stopped.

"We're here!" she cried. "Jessie's house!" Emily was as excited as a little girl at Christmas as she stepped to the ground. "Mrs. Wheeler," she said, "would you mind terribly if I ran ahead and knocked on the door? Oh, I hope Jessie's going to be as glad to see me as I am her!"

"You run ahead," Mrs. Wheeler said. "The driver will bring our bags and—"

"Thanks!" Emily interrupted and ran under the winter-bare maple trees, leaped upon the small wooden front porch, and excitedly knocked on the door. She heard footsteps coming, and she closed her eyes for a brief, silent prayer of gratitude.

Emily's eyes opened as the door swung open. She stared in surprise. It wasn't her friend Jessie or her mother, but a handsome young man in a blue uniform.

"Brice?" she exclaimed in disbelief.

"Emily!" He swung the door wide and grinned happily at her. "You've grown! You're a pretty young woman! Come in! Come in." He turned and shouted into the house, "Mother! Jessie! Emily's come home!"

SOMETIMES HOME REALLY ISN'T

Joyful tears flowed freely as Emily, Jessie, and her mother hugged one another and all tried to talk at once. Through misty eyes, Emily saw Brice standing close by, his gaze never leaving her. It was only when mother and daughter stepped back to look at Emily and exclaim how grown-up she was that Emily introduced Mrs. Wheeler.

They warmly welcomed her as the sliding pocket doors behind them parted and the prettiest girl Emily had ever seen stuck her head through the opening. Her dress fell to about two inches above the floor in the style popular with older teens. Emily guessed she was about seventeen. She asked with a smile, "What's all the excitement?"

Jessie cried, "Oh, Pru! This is Emily Lodge! I've told you about her. Mrs. Wheeler is her chaperon. Emily, this is Prudence Teague, recently from Chicago. A year ago, she and her parents moved onto the old Smith farm to the east, but she and Jessie spend a lot of time together over here."

At the mention of her name, Emily noticed the other girl's smile vanish and be replaced by a slight frown. She looked from Emily to Brice. Quickly, Prudence flashed him a smile that showed a dimple in her left cheek. "Brice, I'm ready for our buggy ride."

"Oh," he replied, "you don't mind waiting awhile, do you? I want to hear all about Emily's experiences in the South. Sit down, everyone. I'll stoke the fire."

Emily caught a flicker of annoyance in Prudence's eyes, which were the most unusual Emily had ever seen. They were green with a golden tint. Her tiny mouth puckered briefly before she said, "That's fine, Brice."

Emily's eyes followed him as he turned and limped toward the open fireplace. He was quite slender and handsome at nearly six feet tall, with sandy-colored hair and the start of a reddish mustache. Emily had never seen him limp before, indicating that he had been wounded again and sent home to recuperate.

Emily sat down and shifted her gaze to Prudence. Her dress was without ornamentation, except for buttons going up from her tiny waist over a full bosom to the closed neckline. She wore a hairnet over dark hair that was parted in the middle. Emily sensed that Prudence resented Brice not going off with her right away.

Brice picked up a poker and crouched in front of the fireplace but turned to look over his shoulder. His pale blue eyes focused on Emily. "Tell us," he said. "How was your trip, and are you back to stay?"

Jessie said, "Why didn't you write us to expect you?"

Emily turned her eyes away from Prudence, but not before she gave Emily a stabbing look of disapproval.

Uh-oh! She thought. *I don't think she likes me!*

Suddenly Emily sensed that her homecoming was not going to be quite what she had dreamed about.

★ ★ ★ ★ ★

After picking up Herb Hunter's story and returning to Richmond, Gideon left Zeb at the hospital and went on to the *Sun*. Max was again at the front desk.

"It's about time you got back, Tugwell," he greeted Gideon sarcastically. "You got Hunter's story all right?"

"Here." Gideon handed it across the desk and started to turn to leave.

"That's all?" Max asked. "Where's the story you wrote for me?"

There was such a taunting tone to Max's words that Gideon sharply whirled around. "I didn't write one because I'm not going to let you steal any more stories from me!"

"Oooh! Temper, temper, Tugwell!" Max said mockingly. "Now,

either you turn in stories to me, or I'll find a way to get you fired! Understand?"

Indignant anger erupted in Gideon. He clenched his teeth and struggled to control the sharp reply that leaped to mind. He had come with the intention of simply dropping off Hunter's story and leaving quickly to avoid a confrontation. But now, as it had been for years with William Lodge of Briarstone, Gideon had taken enough. He hadn't quite been able to beat William, but he had tried and William had finally quit picking on him.

With great self-control Gideon said, "Max, there are some things worse than a thief, but when my writing is stolen, a part of me is also stolen! Now, I'm only going to tell you this one time: You steal anything else from me, and it'll be the last you steal from anyone!"

Gideon noticed a flicker of fear in the other boy's eyes and took advantage of that. Without another word, Gideon whirled around and left the newspaper, hoping his bluff had worked.

★　★　★　★　★

After escaping from Cobb in the river bottom, Nat had run back to the Yateses' home to report the incident. Cobb was gone when Mr. Yates and Nat returned to recover the hog. The incident wasn't reported to the sheriff. It would have been a black man's word against a white man's; even Barley Cobb's word might be believed over Nat's.

The Yateses never again allowed Nat to work alone. Often in the evening, before he retired to the small but comfortable freedmen's quarters, the Yateses invited him into their home.

One evening, Nat sat in his benefactors' kitchen, listening to Mr. and Mrs. Yates's stirring stories about famous black leaders. Although Nat would be speaking to Mrs. Yates's friends who didn't own slaves, they were Confederates who might favor slavery. Some of them might be hostile toward him.

Mrs. Yates suggested, "Start out by telling them what a typical day was like for you. I'm sure they have no idea how cruel life is for millions of slaves."

"I'm willing to try, Mrs. Yates," Nat replied, "but it was nothing exciting. In fact, it was very dull. When I was about seven, I had to carry firewood into the kitchen and take water buckets to the field slaves. Before dawn, they had to feed the livestock, eat a fatback and cornmeal breakfast, be in the fields by sunrise, and work until dark. But they couldn't rest or even eat until tools had been put away, the stock fed, and other chores done. Nobody wants to hear about that."

"On the contrary," Mr. Yates said. "We farmers work hard, but we have something to show for our labors at the end of the day. What do slaves have?"

"Nothing," Nat admitted. "We had only what clothes the master gave us, a crowded cabin to sleep in, and hard, hard work. Slaves can't have any will of their own but are entirely under the control of others."

Nat's voice began to rise as the remembered injustices poured into his mind. "Sometimes," he continued, "a couple might choose to be husband and wife, but they could still be sold apart or have their children sold away, like my family!"

He didn't mean to get emotional, but he felt tears forming as images of his mother, sister, and brothers flashed into his mind. His head dropped into his hands.

He was aware of Mr. Yates's chair squeaking as he arose. Nat felt the farmer's calloused hand rest on his shoulder just as a knock came at the front door. Nat didn't raise his head.

He heard Mrs. Yates say quietly, "I'll get it, Baruch. You stay with him."

Nat roused himself, ashamed of having shown so much emotion. "I'd better go to my quarters," he said.

"Not yet," Mr. Yates said. "We'd like to hear more, and maybe whoever's at the door would, too."

"If you don't mind, I don't want your friends to see me right now. But tell your wife I'll come speak to her friends whatever night she chooses." He headed for the back door but stopped when Mrs. Yates returned and called after him.

"Nat, please wait! This concerns you."

He turned to see Mrs. Yates with John Fletcher.

She said to him, "Tell them why you're here."

★ ★

Nodding, the Tugwells' hired man said, "Dilly, the freedman who's been helping us, has disappeared."

Nat involuntarily sucked in his breath, barely hearing startled exclamations from Mr. and Mrs. Yates. Nat was sure he knew what had happened to Dilly, and his own narrow escape from Barley Cobb leaped to mind.

Fletcher explained, "He might have been frightened away by Cobb, but I'm pretty sure Dilly was kidnapped while working alone on the fence near the swamp. I found two sets of tracks leading into there."

"Barley Cobb!" Mrs. Yates exclaimed.

"Must have been," Fletcher agreed. "But I lost their tracks in the swamp. I hate to say it, but I suspect Cobb's going to sell him back into slavery."

Nat said with deep feeling, "I'm so sorry! Is there anything that can be done to help him?"

"I joined the sheriff in searching around the edge of the swamp, but we didn't find where they came out."

Mrs. Yates urged, "John, tell my husband and Nat what you have in mind."

Nat's stomach twisted violently because he knew why Fletcher was there.

"Martha—Mrs. Tugwell—and I wondered if we could borrow Nat for a while. I hate to ask that, but the only alternative is to bring Gideon home from Richmond to help run the farm. Is that all right, Mr. Yates?"

"Certainly. I've got other hired help besides Nat, but if Dilly can't be replaced and Gideon has to come home, that could be the end of his dream to become a writer."

Nat thought, *If I go to the Tugwells', it won't always be possible to be near Fletcher. So if Cobb caught me alone near the swamp, he could force me to follow him just like poor Dilly.*

Nat sighed. *I want Gideon to succeed, but what about the risk to my dream?* Nat forced the thought away and silently told himself, *I owe my freedom to all these people, so I can't refuse.* He asked, "When do I start?"

★ ★

★　★　★　★　★

Gideon had not been to see Mrs. Stonum or Hannah since returning from his balloon ride with Zeb, so one evening Gideon stopped by the widow's home. She and Hannah greeted him warmly.

Hannah asked, "At the place where I work, one of the girls said there was a rumor that some war balloon got away near Fredericksburg. That was about the time you were there. Did you see it?"

"See it?" Gideon repeated. "Zeb and I were in it!"

"You were?" Hannah exclaimed. "Tell us about it."

"Yes, by all means!" Mrs. Stonum added.

"Well," Gideon began and told the story as a writer, first hooking their interest and then skillfully peeling a verbal onion, one layer at a time. When he neared the climax, Hannah's eyes were wide.

"Oh mercy!" she exclaimed. "How did you escape?"

Gideon enjoyed the rapt response from both Hannah and the widow, so he made a dramatic pause.

Mrs. Stonum leaned forward in her chair. "Well? Then what happened?"

Gideon explained, "The wind changed direction, so we drifted back over our own Confederate lines. By then, the air had cooled so much that the balloon was coming down fast. Our basket snagged on the top of a tree, and the balloon slowly collapsed on the tree and the ground. Zeb and I climbed down, and that was it."

"Oh my!" Mrs. Stonum exclaimed. "Both of you could have been killed!"

Hannah heaved a sigh of relief. "Oh, I'm glad you're safe, Gideon!" She added quickly, "I mean, both of you."

"Zeb and I both said a real quick prayer after we got down," Gideon declared. "Then when we saw the balloon's owner running toward us, we thought he was going to be really mad. But after he found out we were all right and the balloon was, too, he calmed down."

"What a story you can write about that!" Mrs. Stonum declared. "The editor should really like it."

★　★

Shaking his head, Gideon explained, "I'm not going to write it."

"Why not?" Hannah exclaimed. "It's a great story."

Gideon didn't want to embarrass himself by admitting that Max had been submitting Gideon's stories to the editor as his own, and Gideon didn't know how to handle that. He said, "Thanks, but I just can't, and I can't say why."

He watched Hannah and Mrs. Stonum exchange puzzled looks, but neither pressed him further.

"Oh, Gideon!" Hannah exclaimed, jumping up. "A private carrier brought a letter for you today." She got it from a small parlor table and handed it over to him.

"Thanks," he said. "It's from my mother." He read the first couple of lines, then involuntarily sucked in his breath at her next words: *Emily has gone back to Illinois to live and should be there by the time you receive this letter.*

Gideon had always known that Emily planned to do that, but now that she was really gone, he suddenly had a terrible aching feeling deep inside.

"Bad news?" Hannah anxiously asked.

Sighing, Gideon repeated his mother's words, then hurriedly excused himself and left to be alone with his thoughts.

★ ★ ★ ★ ★

A light snow fell on Friday when Mrs. Wheeler went on to Chicago, but it had cleared the next morning when Emily and Jessie started for the short walk to see the house where Emily had grown up. As the snow crunched underfoot, Emily said, "I'm glad you understood that I didn't want anyone else along, in case I lose control of my emotions when I see the old place."

Jessie pushed her brunette ringlets back under her stocking cap. "I think you're wise to do that."

There was something in Jessie's voice that made Emily glance questioningly at her.

She added quickly, "I know how I'd feel if I had lost my entire family in our house."

Emily decided to change the subject. "Why won't your brother talk about why he limps?"

"Because this is the fourth time he's been wounded, and he's afraid the next time he might get killed."

Emily's hand flew to her throat. "What?"

"You saw him in the Richmond hospital when he almost lost his arm from the first wound. At Sharpsburg—I believe they call it Antietam in the South—he was hit three times in a few minutes. One ball grazed his ribs, another went through his right bicep, and a third took a chunk out of his left leg, making him limp. There were no broken bones, but he's afraid next time he won't be so lucky."

Emily's stomach lurched at the terrible thought. She fell silent and hurried to keep up with Jessie's long-legged stride. From the time Emily had arrived, everyone had endlessly talked about how things were before the war, about people they knew, things they used to do. However, it had not been the happy experience Emily had expected, because Prudence seemed to always be present, morning and evening.

Emily asked, "Why doesn't Prudence like me?"

Jessie's brown eyes showed surprise. "You don't know?"

"No. How could I?"

"She resents the attention my brother gives you."

"He doesn't pay any more attention to me than when I lived here. He always teased us, like a big brother."

"It's changed, Em. In the time you've been gone, you've grown into a young woman, and Brice can't seem to keep his eyes off of you. Pru doesn't like that."

"But I haven't changed toward Brice," Emily protested. "He's your brother and my friend."

"After he was wounded this time and sent home to recuperate, he told us about seeing you when he was a cavalryman in Virginia."

"We did accidentally run into each other. The first time, he saved me from possibly being shamed when I stumbled across some of his soldiers at a river. Later, I found him wounded in the hospital and helped nurse him."

★ ★

"What about the time he was an escaped prisoner of war and you got your friends the Tugwells to hide him from the Rebels?"

"I found Brice unconscious from fever, so what else could I do but help him in any way I could? That is no reason for Prudence not to like me."

"Brice informed all of us that he had repeatedly told you he was going to marry you when you grew up."

"He was joking!" Emily exclaimed with a little laugh.

"Maybe," Jessie conceded, "but I noticed Pru's face when he said that. I'm afraid she thinks he was serious."

Emily fell silent. *Things have changed*, she realized. *Coming home isn't what I expected it to be.*

Jessie broke into Emily's musing. "There's still one more thing we haven't told you. Mother, Brice, and I thought it best not to say anything until you could see for yourself."

Something in her best friend's voice made Emily glance sharply at her. "See what for myself?"

"You'll see when we top that little knoll."

★　★

BAD NEWS FROM HOME

Emily was not prepared for the shock of what she saw. She gazed in horror at what had once been her childhood home. The roof had been partially burned, windows were broken out, and the barn had collapsed. All the smaller outbuildings sagged from neglect, except the outhouse, which leaned precariously backward. High brush had overrun the yard and the once neatly tended fields.

"What happened?" she exclaimed in a shocked whisper.

Jessie explained. "After you moved away, the man who bought the property was lazy. He didn't take care of the place, there was a roof fire, and he abandoned everything. Some wild boys broke the windows."

"Come on!" Emily grabbed Jessie's hand and started running down the small mound toward what had once been a gracious two-story house filled with memories.

Sick at heart, Emily ran across the front yard, where she had often played in the colorful autumn leaves from the now-barren maple trees. In deepening anguish, she carefully stepped upon the broken boards of the front porch. Easing past the sagging front door, where the stench of fire lingered, she looked inside and moaned.

She felt Jessie's comforting hand on her arm. "I'm sorry, Em. But we knew you'd want to see it."

Too stricken to reply, Emily entered the long, dark hallway to the silent and empty parlor. Her grandfather had been laid out there after he died. The upright organ Emily's mother had practiced on for Sunday services at Old Bethel Church was blackened and useless. Still, in memory, Emily could hear Mother's sweet voice singing those grand old hymns. Tears flowed freely as Emily moved down the gloomy hallway with bedrooms on either side and wind moaning through the broken panes.

Jessie sounded as if she were also going to weep when she quietly urged, "Say something, Em."

She managed to brokenly whisper, "This was my room."

"I remember the times I stayed over with you. This time of year, we'd heat a sadiron behind the potbellied stove, take the handle off the iron, wrap it in a heavy cloth, and put it by our feet to keep warm. Remember?"

Emily smiled through her tears. "Yes, and we'd heat our pillows behind the stove and run down the cold hall with my mother carrying the lamp. Remember the way the shadows raced ahead of the light, and when she had tucked us in and took the lamp away, how dark it was?"

Jessie urged, "Try to remember all the good times before . . . before the sad things happened."

Emily nodded, but the tears flowed faster. "Why, Jessie?" she cried in anguish. "Why are they all dead and I alone am left alive? Why?"

Jessie slipped her arms around Emily's shoulders and pulled her close. "Everyone I know has asked that. The best answer we ever got was from the pastor. He said, 'Things happen that none of us will ever understand. Perhaps some people's reason for being ends sooner than others.' So maybe, Emily, God has something special for you to do, and that's why you're still here."

Shaking her head violently, Emily protested, "My brothers were younger than I! Children! How could their reason for being be over so soon?"

"Nobody knows. The only thing we do know is that you're still here, so the Lord must have a reason."

"What reason?" Emily cried. "What would I do that maybe my parents or brothers couldn't have done better?"

Jessie gently suggested, "Why don't you ask God?"

For a long moment, Emily remained silent, thinking. Then she

★ ★

nodded. "I believe I will. Let's go back to your house where I can be alone for a while."

★　★　★　★　★

When Nat entered the small frame church where the Yateses and Tugwells worshiped, he instantly felt the hostility of the farmers' wives. He wondered why they had come, unless it was to challenge him. He wished that he hadn't agreed to speak to them about his life in slavery.

Mrs. Yates had told Nat that none of them owned slaves. However, they were all loyal to the Confederate cause, and Nat was a threat to their culture and way of life. He was a freed slave and represented to them the four million slaves who would also be free if the Union won the war and Lincoln's Emancipation Proclamation was carried out.

Like most slaves, Nat had learned to hide his true feelings from white people. He pretended not to notice the disapproval in these women's eyes, the stern set of their jaws, and the way some crossed their arms in silent rejection of what he might say.

He automatically assumed the attitude expected by white folks by keeping his eyes downcast as Mrs. Yates introduced him. He wasn't afraid, but he did not want to disappoint his benefactress. He had prepared himself by recalling his mother's frequent admonition: *"Winning is in the mind and not the muscles."*

When the introduction was complete and he stood, there was not even polite applause. Taking a risk, Nat raised his gaze and slowly met every woman's eyes before he said a word. By then, his bold move had created surprise and perhaps offense, resulting in a stillness in the small church.

"I understand that all of you are mothers," he began quietly, remembering the manner in which Brother Tynes had started his sermon. "I know some of your sons are away fighting the war. But they think of you and write when they can. You live in hope that they will all return to you someday, and you'll be together again."

Nat paused, catching a sudden glistening in the eyes of a heavyset woman in the front row. "Nearly two years ago, my mother, my three brothers, my little sister, and I were put on the

★　★

auction block and sold apart as casually as your husbands sell your livestock and offspring. But unlike animals, slave mothers and children have deep feelings, just as you and your children have. For slaves, the pain of separation never goes away. Almost always, slave mothers and children never see each other again."

The audience was touched. Nat sensed it from the slight shifting of feet and squirming sounds. Nat continued, relating the bitter memories of slavery but without condemning anyone. He became more animated in body and tone, his voice rising in imitation of Tynes. But Nat quickly realized he was awkward at it.

He began to falter, would start a sentence, stop, then try again. Fear oozed into him as the white audience reacted differently from the slaves at the secret woods meetings.

Perhaps, he warned himself, *they feel threatened to have a slave raise his voice in their presence.*

Nat realized that he would have to just be himself. He abandoned Tynes' style and continued in firm, quiet tones, telling of his life as a slave. He was quickly aware that his audience was more comfortable and relaxed with his subdued tone. The entire group leaned forward as one.

Nat told of his life from birth through various escape attempts. A hush fell over everyone as he recounted how he had found his mother, little sister, and one brother and headed them toward freedom in Canada. He was still hoping to find his two youngest brothers, Amos and Gabe.

He paused before adding, "I paid a price for my escapes, but I would do it again and pay the cost again." He abruptly yanked up his shirt, saying, "It cost me these stripes to try finding my family."

He turned his bare back so the spider web of ugly, raised welts showed where he had been repeatedly whipped. Now there were hideous scars where flesh had been ripped and blood had flowed before saltwater had been thrown on the raw flesh to increase the pain.

He heard the startled gasps and dropped his shirt. He turned and faced the mothers. They had changed. Arms were no longer defiantly crossed. There were no looks of resentment. Instead, tears flowed freely down many cheeks. There was much dabbing at eyes and discreet sniffling.

"Now, mothers," Nat said softly, again meeting every pair of eyes, "be thankful that your children do not pay the price of chains and slavery. In time, I hope and pray that you will understand the incredible gift of freedom that all of you enjoy. I now join you in that freedom and hope that someday all of God's children will be free."

He bowed slightly. "Thank you for your kind attention," he said and sat down.

There was no applause, only silence broken by a few low sobs and delicate sniffling. Nat had a sinking feeling he had been wrong; he had not been as effective as he thought. With a sense of failure, he believed that he had not honored Mrs. Yates with a successful presentation.

Then the heavyset woman in the front row who had first shown a tear clapped once, twice, then again. Slowly, gently, her hands came together, creating an echo in the room. Another woman in the back joined in the clapping, but her pace was harder and faster. Abruptly, spontaneously, the entire audience rose as one. The applause rolled harder and faster until Nat dropped his eyes to hide the moisture that erupted there.

★ ★ ★ ★ ★

That night, after a frustrating day of praying as Jessie had suggested, an overwhelming need drove Emily to talk to Jessie's mother. Emily found her alone, sewing by lamplight in the parlor. The room was invitingly warm from the potbellied stove in the corner as Emily accepted Mrs. Barlow's invitation to sit down.

Emily began, "I miss my mother so terribly much! I miss her even more after seeing our old house today."

"My dear Emily," Mrs. Barlow said, sticking her needle into a pincushion and laying the work aside. "Every girl needs a mother while growing up, especially when she is nearing young womanhood with the questions that are part of that time of life. I deeply regret that your mother can't be with you, but you're like a daughter to me. Would you like to talk?"

★ ★

For several heartbeats, Emily remained thoughtfully silent. Finally she said, "Ever since I left here to go live with my uncle Silas and his family in Virginia, I have longed to be back home. I prayed incessantly, and I tried for months to get passes through the lines. The first time I actually got the passes and started north but was turned back because of a battle."

Mrs. Barlow silently waited while Emily took a breath and then continued.

"When I got back to Briarstone, my friend Gideon suggested that maybe God wanted me there for some reason. I didn't want to hear that; I just wanted to come home. But now that I'm here, it's not the same. In fact, it's not my home anymore, and that breaks my heart!"

Emily's voice broke, and she turned away to hide the unwelcome tears that misted her vision.

Mrs. Barlow said gently, "There comes a time in each of our lives when we must put the past behind and move on. Oh, it's nice to sometimes come back to the house where we grew up, with its wonderful memories of people we loved. But even that has been taken from you, and I can only guess why."

Emily turned around, feeling tears on her eyelashes. "Tell me why! I need something that makes sense!"

Mrs. Barlow explained, "I believe God is preparing you for something special. You have been sorely tried in the crucible of life, and your faith is now stronger. I suspect you will need that strength—strength beyond your own very strong-willed and self-reliant nature. You will need the Lord for whatever lies ahead."

Emily asked, "Are you trying to frighten me?"

"Far from it! I want you to know that you are capable of whatever task God put you on earth to do. And I will do everything I can to help you, my dear."

"But don't you have some idea of what I'm to do?"

"No, Emily. I don't have a clue. But I'm confident that the Union is going to win this terrible war. When it's over, you'll be a young woman, ready for life."

Emily asked, "Why do you think all my family died except me?"

"The Book of Isaiah tells us that God's ways and thoughts are higher than ours," Mrs. Barlow replied. "I believe your situation falls in that category, for I'm convinced that God has a plan for every life. But it's up to each individual to accept or reject that plan. Emily, are you willing to accept His plan instead of yours?"

Emily protested, "How can I answer that when I don't know what plan God might have in mind for me?"

"Ask Him," she replied. "Ask in faith, believing that He will answer. But be prepared in case it isn't what you want. You won't be forced to accept, but I'm sure it will be more rewarding than you can imagine."

Emily slowly nodded. "I'll do that," she said.

★　★　★　★　★

Nat eagerly waited for Mr. and Mrs. Yates to tell him what they had declined to tell him until after he talked to the women's group.

Mrs. Yates began, "I don't have to tell you what a great impact your talk had on my friends. Some privately admitted to me that they came prepared to dislike you, but instead, they were so impressed that they want you to speak to other groups."

Nat said, "I don't know about that."

"Think about it," Mrs. Yates urged. "Now, as my husband and I told you before, we have a suggestion that we wanted to withhold from you until we heard your talk."

The usually quiet Mr. Yates smiled and said, "We believe the North will win the war, and that means there will be a new South. It will be devastated by then, and many white men now fighting will not return to rebuild."

Mrs. Yates added, "Four million slaves will be free, and they'll be like sheep without a shepherd. My husband and I, who both oppose the war and slavery, believe that in the new South the time will come when a former slave can vote and even be elected to public office."

Nat almost laughed, the idea was so preposterous, but he controlled himself.

Mr. Yates said, "We believe you should consider using your lit-

★　★

eracy and your speaking ability to become a lawyer and perhaps someday run for public office!"

Nat stared in disbelief, but he didn't feel like laughing anymore.

Maybe I could do that, he told himself, then added soberly, *if I can keep Barley Cobb from grabbing me and reselling me into slavery!*

★   ★   ★   ★   ★

A week later, with Zeb on a pass from the hospital, Gideon and he stopped by to see Mrs. Stonum and Hannah, where two letters were waiting for Gideon. While Zeb told the woman and girl about his experiences of going into battle armed only with a drum, Gideon first opened Emily's letter because he hadn't heard from her since before she left Briarstone.

It was a friendly letter, recounting her trip north and staying with the Barlow family. Then Gideon read a line that made his heart seem to stop.

> *You remember Jessie's older brother, Brice? Well, he's been wounded again and is recuperating at home. It's so good to see him, as well as Jessie and her mother.*

Gideon closed his eyes at the remembered pain of Brice's boasts that he was someday going to marry Emily. To hide his surging emotions, Gideon shoved Emily's letter into his pocket without reading the rest. He turned his eyes on his mother's words.

After the usual *We are well and hope you are the same*, she added, *Barley Cobb has either scared Dilly away or kidnapped him. John Fletcher and your little brother are being helped out temporarily by Nat because they can't handle the farm by themselves.*

Gideon's pulse speeded up as his eyes jumped ahead to the next line. He read it aloud to himself.

" 'I hate to write this, Gideon, but when Nat has to return to helping the Yateses, then I'm afraid you'll have to come home or we'll lose the farm!' "

★   ★

DREAMS AT RISK

Gideon was so shocked over his mother's letter that he wasn't aware he had made any sound until Hannah spoke.

"Something wrong, Gideon?"

In sudden agony of soul, he replied, "Mama says I may have to come home to help save our farm."

"Oh, Gideon!" Hannah exclaimed, leaving Zeb and Mrs. Stonum to lightly touch his arm. "I'm so sorry!"

Mrs. Stonum added, "So am I. I know how much you want to stay here and succeed as a writer."

No, you don't! Gideon thought, fighting the bitter disappointment that seized him. *Nobody can know how much it means for me to become a good writer!*

Zeb declared, "If you go home, maybe I can get a pass to go with you. Wouldn't that be great, Gideon?"

Gideon was too stricken to sense how eager his young friend was to see a real home and family. "Yes," Gideon replied without enthusiasm. "I know what I must do for my family, but it means the end of my dreams...."

"No, it doesn't!" the widow said emphatically. She crossed to face him. "Didn't your mother's letter say that you *might* have to come home?"

Gideon glanced again at the letter. "Yes. *Might.*"

"See?" Mrs. Stonum's tone carried encouragement. "And even if you did have to, it might only be for a short time. A delay, but not the end. You have talent, Gideon, and the newspaper training will help you develop it. So don't give up, no matter what happens!"

"She's right, Gideon!" Hannah exclaimed. "You've risked a lot for that dream, so you mustn't quit trying."

Feeling a little better, Gideon slowly nodded.

Zeb asked, "Who was your other letter from?"

Gideon's thoughts returned to Emily's letter. In pain, he recalled her words. *"You remember Jessie's older brother, Brice. . . . It's so good to see him. . . ."*

Gideon realized that Emily would never have written that if she had any idea how disturbing it would be to him. *I didn't even realize that myself*, he thought. *I don't know why I let it bother me so much!*

"Well," Zeb prompted, "who was it from?"

Gideon took a slow, deep breath to gain control of his emotions so his voice would not betray his feelings. "Oh, just my friend Emily. I haven't finished reading it, but so far, she told about being back home where she's wanted to be for so long."

Gideon turned to Mrs. Stonum. "If you don't mind, I think I should go back to my room and answer my mother."

Zeb said, "I'll go to the hospital and see if they'll give me a pass to go home with you, since you're like my brother. Your mother won't mind, will she?"

Gideon fondly roughed his young friend's hair. "No, of course not, Zeb. If I don't go home for about a month, maybe you could spend Christmas with us."

"Christmas!" Zeb exclaimed, his eyes lighting up. "I haven't had a real Christmas since my folks died years ago! We'll have so much fun, won't we?"

"Sure," Gideon dully replied. "It'll be a great Christmas."

★　★　★　★　★

When Nat, Mrs. Tugwell, her children, and John Fletcher returned from Sunday-morning services, they found the corral gate had accidentally been left open and the family cow was gone. After quickly changing clothes and taking a couple of ropes, Nat, Fletcher, and Gideon's brother Ben followed her tracks in the

★　★

snow. A strong wind pushed them along as they circled a dense stand of trees near the swamp.

"I knew it!" Ben declared, his voice cracking as it had been doing since just before he turned twelve. "Her tracks show she's headed straight for the swamp."

Nat's skin crawled at the word as he vividly recollected the terror he and the slave girl Sarah had felt in trying to escape from Briarstone. In a frantic effort to reach the local Underground Railroad station, he and Sarah had struggled through the treacherous swamp, hotly pursued by Barley Cobb and his hounds.

Fletcher pushed his hat up with the stub of his left wrist where he had lost the hand in battle. "I can guess why. Hear that bawling from somewhere in the swamp?"

Ben cocked his head to better hear from upwind of the sound. "Wild cattle! She's headed straight for them! I hope she didn't get through our fence line."

"Your hope comes too late, Ben," Fletcher said. "I can see where she broke through. I just hope we can catch up to her before she joins up with . . . listen!"

Even with the wind blowing from the hunters to the swamp, Nat heard muted baying. Gooseflesh erupted along his forearms. "Dogs! Cobb's running his hounds in there!"

Fletcher faced Nat. "We can't risk having you go in there. Cobb's hounds are especially trained to follow certain scents, and they may have already gotten yours. You stay here. Cobb won't bother Ben and me."

"I'd rather be with you two," Nat protested.

"It's not safe," Fletcher said firmly. "You go on back to the house. Ben and I can handle the cow."

Reluctantly, Nat watched them until they were swallowed up in the great tangle of trees and brush. He turned back, thinking about the Yateses' suggestion that he become an attorney and maybe run for office if the North won the war. But his main goal remained unchanged: to find his two brothers. He also wanted to repay his benefactors for the money they had paid for his freedom.

So, he wondered, *how can I even think of becoming a lawyer with all I really want to do?*

★ ★

He was circling the stand of trees on the Tugwell property when he heard the unmistakable twin clicks as a double-barrel gun was brought back to full cock.

"Don't move!" Cobb called, stepping from behind a large tree trunk, with the ugly weapon leveled at Nat.

★　★　★　★　★

Emily felt strange after Jessie left on a sleigh ride with her brother and Prudence. They had invited Emily to go along, but she knew from Pru's attitude that she didn't want Emily to accept. She had also noticed that Jessie seemed a little cool toward her.

Since Emily had no money to pay for her keep, she washed dishes and did other household chores for her host family. Emily poured hot water from the kettle into a dishpan and began washing the midday dishes, when Mrs. Barlow entered the kitchen.

Emily said, "Do you have a moment to talk?"

Jessie's mother picked up a dish towel and reached for a wet plate. "Of course. What can I do for you?"

Emily tried to tactfully phrase her question. "Is it my imagination, or has Jessie changed a little since I last saw her?"

"Of course she has, Emily. So have you. That's only natural, especially when good friends are apart for such a long time. Friendships change. But she still loves you very much. She also likes Prudence."

Emily nodded. "I noticed that."

"Shortly after Pru moved here, Jessie got Pru to write Brice. Even though there's no regular mail between North and South, their letters eventually got through. When he came home to recuperate from his wounds, the three started going places together, as just now. But Jessie still considers you a good friend."

But not "best" friends anymore, Emily thought. She said somberly, "I see." She quickly added, "I don't want to wear out my welcome here, so I'm going to look for another place to stay in exchange for doing housework."

"You're not going to wear out your welcome, Emily! You're like family."

"Thank you, but I am old enough to realize that tensions can arise, even among family, and I don't want that to happen with us."

Mrs. Barlow placed the dried dish in an open overhead cupboard. "You needn't worry about that. In fact, we would all be upset if you left—even Brice."

Emily raised an eyebrow. "Thanks, but I don't think Prudence would be upset."

"That's because she sees the way my son keeps looking at you."

Emily blinked. "What?"

"Haven't you noticed, Emily? Why, if you were sixteen instead of almost fourteen, I'm sure Brice would want to court you."

"Me?" Emily's tone showed her surprise. "He's like a big brother!"

"By the time this war is over, you'll be a grown woman. Mark my word, Emily, by then you won't think of him as a big brother."

Emily shook her golden tresses. "He is very nice looking and has always been good to me, but—"

"I know," Mrs. Barlow interrupted. "You aren't yet thinking about a beau. So forget what I said, because if Pru has her way, she'll eventually be Mrs. Brice Barlow."

Emily heaved a heavy sigh and made up her mind to move. "Next Sunday at church, I plan to ask around for someone who will trade what I can do for room and board."

Mrs. Barlow hugged Emily. "I hadn't wanted to say anything for fear that you'd misunderstand my motive. But Mrs. Higgins just this morning asked me if I thought you'd like to help her with housework and tutor her three children in exchange for room and board."

"I'm glad you mentioned it," Emily said sincerely. "I'll talk to her next Sunday."

★　★　★　★　★

Nat's eyes shifted from the deadly twin muzzles aimed at his heart. His blood pounded so loudly he could hear it inside his head as he faced the slave catcher.

Cobb's small eyes glittered with pleasure when he spoke through an untrimmed and tobacco-stained beard. "Fooled ye

★　★

ag'in, didn't I, black boy? Ye ain't right smart in the haid, or you'd a learnt from down in the river bottom. Ye cain't outfox an ol' hunter like me."

All of Nat's thoughts about finding his brother and possibly becoming a lawyer vanished in the presence of the man who would resell him into slavery. *Unless*, he thought, *I can get out of this—and fast!*

He said the first thing that popped into his mind. "I know how you did it," Nat said quietly. "You've been watching the house, and you let the cow out."

"How did ye know that, boy? I was plumb keerful to not leave no tracks. I walked on the fence boards to the gate to open it an' then went back the same way! Then I circled wide in the field, away from that ol' cow so I didn't leave nary a track in the snow!"

Heartened by his guess, Nat replied, "While we were at church, you tied your hounds downwind in the swamp so that when we went looking for the cow, the dogs would catch my scent and start baying."

"Think yore so blasted smart, don't ye?" Cobb growled. "Well, how do ye recken I figured that one-handed man and the boy would leave ye behind? An' me to be a-waitin' here fer ye to come back alone?"

Nat thought quickly. "Because you knew that Mr. Fletcher wouldn't let me go near those dogs."

Cobb said grudgingly, "Ye got more smarts than most o' yore kind; I give ye that. But ye cain't git up early enough in the mawrnin' to outsmart me. Now, walk over here and turn around. This time, ye'll wear my handirons all the way down the muddy Mississippi!"

Nat hesitated, weighing his options of being blasted where he stood or surrendering to bondage again. Suddenly, from the woods behind the slave catcher, a voice commanded, "Drop it, Cobb, and don't turn around!"

Nat's eyes lifted with his spirits. "Mr. Fletcher!"

Cobb froze in place, then slowly shook his head. "Fletcher, I seen ye a-walkin' across the field jist minutes ago, an' ye didn't have no gun. So I'm not—"

★ ★

"My pistol was under my coat," Fletcher interrupted. "If you doubt me, just try turning around! Now lower that barrel and let both those hammers down real easy."

Nat held his breath because he knew the one-handed man was bluffing. He had no weapon of any kind.

"Last chance, Cobb!" Fletcher said harshly.

Nat anxiously watched Cobb as he slowly lowered the gun barrel toward the ground and eased the hammers down. Nat needed no instruction from Fletcher and took the weapon, quickly handing it to Fletcher.

Cobb, realizing he had been tricked, cursed loudly until Fletcher ordered him to stop.

Ben came out from behind a tree where Fletcher had ordered him to stay for safety. "Huzzah, Mr. Fletcher," he cried. "Good thing we found Cobb's tracks and you figured out what he was up to!"

Fletcher nodded and looked at Nat. "You all right?"

"Yes, thanks. I can't ever thank you enough."

"It's not necessary," Fletcher said. "Let's get our prisoner to the house and send for the sheriff."

As they all started toward the Tugwells' small home, Nat realized that he had almost lost his freedom again and possibly his life. Now he had another chance.

★ ★ ★ ★ ★

With a heavy heart, Gideon entered the front door of the *Sun*. He didn't want to tell the editor that he might have to quit and go back to help on the family farm. Nat hoped that Max wasn't at the desk, but he was. It was the first time they'd met since Gideon had stood up to him.

"Max," Gideon said without hesitation, "I have to see Mr. Kerr right away."

"He's out." Max's eyes narrowed suspiciously as he studied Gideon. "So I'll take Hunter's story."

"This has nothing to do with him," Gideon replied, trying to keep his dislike of the narrow-faced boy from showing. "It's personal."

Max's lips curled into a sneer. "I know what you really want! You're going to tell him that I've been taking credit for your stories."

"You mean stealing my stories!" Gideon snapped. "Well, not that it's any of your business, but that's not why I need to see Mr. Kerr. When will he be back?"

"In a week; about the first of December."

Gideon said, "Then I'll leave a note on his desk."

Max leaped from his chair and stepped between Gideon and the inner door. Max placed both hands on his hips and blocked the way. "Nobody goes past me unless I say so."

A rare, sudden surge of anger raced over Gideon so that he felt his face tighten and he clenched his fists. Then he realized that even if he left a note, Max might read it before the editor saw it.

Max's attitude changed. "I'm just doing my job!" he cried, his voice a little trembly. "You want to get me discharged?"

Instantly relenting, Gideon relaxed his face and took a deep breath. "No, I don't. But I've got to talk to Mr. Kerr in person. I'll return when he's back."

Gideon spun on his heels and hurriedly left. Behind him, he heard a heavy sigh of relief. But Gideon was not comforted, because his dream was still at risk.

★ ★

TEACHERS TOUCH
ETERNITY

On the first day of December, Gideon dreaded entering the *Sun* building. It wasn't just that he hoped he wouldn't clash with Max Hassler again. A letter from Gideon's mother had arrived Saturday afternoon by private courier. Her words made his heart ache.

I'm sorry, Gideon, she had written, *but Nat can only stay until the end of December. I hate to say it, but we'll need you back home by then. Could you possibly make it so we could all have Christmas together?*

Gideon was relieved that Max wasn't at the front desk, and the regular bespectacled little man behind the counter promptly admitted him to the editor's office.

As in their first meeting, the stocky Buford Kerr didn't look up from his rolltop desk still overflowing with papers. He seemed to have on the same rumpled clothes as before, including the red braces. His wild graying hair and beard remained untidy.

He finally looked up. "What do you want, Tugwell?"

The old curmudgeon's bluntness affected Gideon as it had when he applied for the job. "Sir," he began in an uncertain voice, "my mother needs me at home, so I've come to say I can only continue to be Mr. Hunter's courier until the end of this—"

Kerr impatiently interrupted, "Why didn't you ever submit anything for me to read? How can I judge if you're ever going to be a writer if you don't write?"

Startled, Gideon blurted, "But I have, sir! My stories were even published. . . ."

"What?" Kerr almost leaped from his squeaking chair to glare at the boy. "You've taken money from this paper for courier work while selling stories to a competitor?"

"Oh no, sir!" Gideon hurriedly exclaimed. "All my writing ran in the *Sun!*" Suddenly realizing that this confession was going to cause trouble, he stopped.

"I hate liars!" Kerr snapped. "I never saw your name on anything, and everything that goes into the editorial side of this paper crosses my desk! So don't lie to me!"

"I'm not!" Gideon's voice trembled. "My stories . . . uh . . . didn't go in under my name."

Kerr studied him in silence before asking, "Am I to assume you're not going to tell me how that happened?"

"I'd rather not, sir."

Kerr's eyes thoughtfully narrowed. "I see."

Impatient to have this over, Gideon blurted, "So will it be all right if I leave before Christmas?"

The editor's eyes were still narrowed as he stared into Gideon's. Finally, Kerr said, "We're coming into our busiest time of the year, so it would be hard for me to find someone dependable to be a courier for Hunter's dispatches. But I'll think about it.

★   ★   ★   ★   ★

Gideon needed to talk to someone, but with Hannah and Mrs. Stonum at work, Gideon went to Chimborazo Hospital to share his tormented thoughts with Zeb.

"Now I'm twice as sick inside," Gideon explained as the boys strolled around the hospital grounds under a threatening sky. "I don't want to give up trying to become a correspondent, yet my family has to come first. But I think the editor believes what I said about my stories, and that means he's suspicious about how they got in the paper. If he asks Max, he'll lie, of course, but that will make Mr. Kerr think I'm the liar."

"What difference does it make?" Zeb asked. "You're going home anyway. I've been waiting to tell you. I can get a pass to go with you. Ain't that great news?"

The eagerness in Zeb's voice made Gideon nod. "Of course it is! We'll have all kinds of fun, too!"

★   ★

Zeb's face sobered. "You're saying the words, but I can see it in your eyes—you're not happy about this."

"Oh, I'm happy about getting to see my family and having you meet them, but I had hoped not to leave here until I had at least succeeded in having some credits."

"But you have! I saved those stories you wrote about me and Hannah! You can show those to your family."

"Thanks, Zeb, but I can't prove that those were really mine."

"Why didn't you tell that mean old editor that Max is stealing your stories?"

Gideon sighed. "I didn't want to get him in trouble."

"Liars and cheats deserve trouble!" Zeb declared. "I'd sure tell what really happened if it was me!"

"I'm probably wrong in keeping quiet, Zeb, but I just can't make myself do that." Gideon shifted away from the sensitive topic. "I'm also concerned about my friend Emily. I wonder if I'll ever see her again."

"You write her, don't you?" Zeb asked.

"Yes, but with no official mail service between North and South, I don't even know if she's getting my letters. I sent her one to wish her a happy birthday, but there's no way of knowing if she got it."

A thought stabbed Gideon. *I wonder if they'll give her a party and Brice will be there.*

Zeb urged, "Tell me again what it will be like for us to have Christmas at your house."

Gideon put his own problems aside, warmly smiled at his friend, and began telling him what to expect.

★ ★ ★ ★ ★

Emily's fourteenth birthday was the first Sunday in December, but nobody had mentioned it; not even Jessie or Gideon. *Well,* Emily silently admitted, *maybe he wrote me but the letter didn't get through yet.*

Emily tried to cheer herself by the fact that Mrs. Higgins and her husband had engaged Emily to live with them in exchange for tutoring their three children. Mrs. Barlow had insisted Emily stay through Christmas.

Even joyful seasonal bells on the horses' harnesses and the Barlows' closed sleigh couldn't cheer Emily during the short ride to Old Bethel Church. Prudence waited outside the small picket fence when Brice reined in the team. Jessie stepped off the sleigh on her own, but Brice helped his mother out, then offered his hand to Emily just as Prudence walked up.

She glared at Emily with eyes cold as the morning air. Emily greeted Prudence, who didn't reply. Emily joined Jessie and her mother in crunching across the snow to the small white church, where long icicles clung to the edge of the roof. Emily glanced back to see Brice help Pru into the sleigh so he could move it across the rural road where horses were tied.

Emily caught an angry snatch of Pru's remark to Brice, "She's only a *child*!"

Emily pretended she hadn't heard, but Jessie, walking beside her, smiled knowingly at Emily. "I think my big brother is getting a tongue-lashing over you."

Mrs. Barlow said, "Never mind, Jessie. Oh, there's Mrs. Watkins. She's being honored today for teaching the same children's Sunday school class for fifty years!"

Emily and Jessie had both attended Mrs. Watkins' class when they were little, so they approached the frail elderly lady standing just inside the outer door. Emily noticed that her blue eyes were still bright as diamonds in a face wrinkled by time, but her smile never seemed to disappear. She had been too ill to attend church the last few weeks, but today she leaned on two canes and warmly greeted everyone.

After Emily and Jessie had gone on to be seated on the hard wooden pews, Emily sighed. "What a wonderful day this must be for Mrs. Watkins! I wonder how many young lives she touched in fifty years of teaching."

Jessie shrugged, so Emily had to wait until the hymns were sung, the pre-Christmas announcements were made, and the part-time pastor, Brother Appleby, took the pulpit.

A tall, rather thin man, with a lock of white hair in the middle

★ ★

of his otherwise bald head, he turned toward Mrs. Watkins seated to his right. Her smile had weakened but had not entirely vanished.

He spoke quietly but with enough force that everyone in the tiny church could hear. "Teachers touch eternity." He made the brief statement and paused, and Emily was strangely stirred by those few words.

"Sister Watkins," the preacher continued, "I remember years ago, when my children were little, you said to me, 'I teach so that heaven will be different.' You have certainly done that, as I'm sure we'll learn someday when we all get to heaven."

Emily had to blink back tears as the pastor turned to face the congregation.

"Brothers and sisters," he said, "there's a reason for that. Paul the apostle tells us that teaching is a God-given talent. Open your Bibles to Ephesians, the fourth chapter, the eleventh verse, and follow along with me as I read."

Emily found the place in the worn, black King James Version that had been her mother's. Jessie leaned closer to see. When the rustling of pages had stopped, the pastor read aloud.

" 'And he'—God—'gave some, apostles; and some, prophets; and some, evangelists; and some, pastors and *teachers*!' " He emphasized the last word, then repeated it loudly. "Teachers! Sister Watkins was not only prepared by God to teach, but she answered that call and has been *faithful*."

Pastor Appleby dragged out the word for emphasis before adding, "Faithful because she chose to be, and we all have choices! I believe this Scripture teaches that God has a purpose for every life, but we are free to choose to accept or reject His plan. Some of you here today have gone on to teach, or will teach, here or other places."

Emily thought that the pastor's eyes briefly rested on her because she had taught Sunday school in this church before moving away. But she couldn't be sure he had singled her out before he spoke again.

"Now, all of you who were ever in Sister Watkins' class, please stand."

★ ★

There was a murmur as Emily, Jessie, and Brice rose to their feet, along with what seemed to Emily to be most of the people in that room. Some were now gray-haired, a few were about six years old, but most were in between.

Some of the older folks still seated began to clap, and the sound grew and swelled until the tiny room was filled with the joyful noise. By now, everyone stood and faced the smiling honoree where she sat leaning forward on her two canes and beaming with eyes brimming with tears.

Emily forgot that it was her birthday and no one seemed to have remembered. She forgot about overhearing Pru's cruel remark to Brice. All the sounds in the room became muted as memories flashed back. She remembered teaching in this church, teaching Gideon and the white overseer's offspring at Briarstone. She knew that even little slave children had listened to her instructions.

Emily's mind speeded up, racing by Mrs. Yates and Mrs. Wheeler urging her to think about becoming a teacher, and not only to teach white children, but blacks if they were no longer slaves. Suddenly Emily's thoughts struck a cold stone wall.

I'd teach anyone, she told herself, *except in the South. I will never return there!*

Instantly, Emily's strong-willed nature solidified those thoughts into a firm resolution. Yet she sensed an immediate internal conflict, so she defiantly tilted her chin up and silently repeated, *Never!*

★ ★ ★ ★ ★

Emily's mental friction over her decision was partly offset by a surprise birthday party that was sprung upon her shortly after she returned to the Barlows' home.

Nobody had forgotten, Emily realized, and she was moved that so many with whom she had gone to school showed up to wish her well. Yet even the laughter of remembered good times could not entirely dissipate the strong feelings aroused at church. Still, she tried to keep those recollections from spoiling the party.

After about an hour, Brice came to where she was sitting

watching everyone and smiling as if she were enjoying everything. He whispered, "What's the matter?"

Emily started to protest that nothing was wrong, but Brice shook his head. "Don't try to fool me, Em. I've been watching you. What's troubling you?"

She glanced across the room and saw Pru watching with narrowed eyes. "Nothing," she said, standing. Then, on impulse, she asked, "Would you tell everyone I don't feel quite well, and I'm going for a walk?"

"In this snow?" Brice protested. "It's too deep."

"I've got to be alone for a while, even if it seems I have no manners."

"Then take my sleigh, Em," Brice urged. "Don't be gone long. I don't want to worry . . . I mean . . . I don't want any of us to worry about you."

"Thanks. I'll be back shortly." She hurried out of the room, driven by something she could not explain.

Emily drove back to Old Bethel and tied up where Brice had this morning. Motivated by the controversy within and drawn by the silent stones in the cemetery, she waded through the snow. She stopped before the large upright marker where her parents and brothers were buried. At first, Emily could not even form her thoughts. She tried to pray but didn't feel comfortable doing that; not with her rebellious attitude.

Slowly, she dropped to her knees, her head down, tears gushing. *Why?* The word screamed in her mind. *Why are all of you dead and I am left alone? Why me? Why?*

She heard only the soft moaning of the wind in the conifer growing by the church's front door and the faint flapping of the wind tugging at her clothes. She was not even aware of the cold seeping through her feet, up her legs, and into her mittened hands.

She didn't know how long she stayed there, but she finally stood and realized how very cold she was. She gently ran her nearly numb hand along the marble shaft, sighed, and left, still with no answers.

★ ★

★ ★ ★ ★ ★

Even though Nat had no way of knowing if the secret slave church services would be held that night, he slipped into the woods. By the fluttering pine torches, he noticed the services hadn't started. A woman was shouting into the barrel, while others stood talking in small groups. Nat was delighted to see Delia, but he was unhappy to see Caesar talking to her.

She waved to Nat and hurried toward him, leaving Caesar frowning in disappointment. Delia was dressed against the cold with old clothes that William's mother and sister had given her.

She greeted Nat with a friendly smile. "I heard," she said, "that you're working for the Tugwells until their son gets back from Richmond."

He grinned at her. "You hear a lot, Delia."

"Certainly do! You know that we sometimes hear things even before the master does through his telegraph. For example, I know that the slave catcher caught you, but you were rescued."

"That's true," Nat admitted a little sheepishly. "I got careless. But thanks to Mr. Fletcher, Cobb ended up in jail for trying to kidnap a freedman."

"You think he's in jail?"

Nat blinked. "Isn't he?"

"No! He escaped. There's a rumor he left the area. You really didn't know about that?"

"No." Nat apprehensively glanced around. "But I don't believe he left the area. I think he's hiding, waiting for a chance to take revenge on me."

"I hope you're wrong, Nat." Delia's tone was soft and warm. "So be careful. Oh, speaking of what's going on, Young Master William caught Levi stealing and sold him down the river. So at least William now knows you were falsely accused. He replaced Levi with Caesar."

Nat glanced to where the other youth sat, his face hard and cold in the torchlight. Nat looked back to Delia. He was eager to tell about his speaking to the women's group and being urged to become a lawyer.

★ ★

Before he could find an opening, Delia said, "The service is about to start, but there's something else I want to tell you. Do you remember when you asked me what I would do if Lincoln frees all of us slaves?"

"Yes, of course. Have you decided?"

"Yes. I'd get an education and—" She broke off as Caesar hurried up and took her arm.

"Time to start," he told her, but his eyes locked firmly on to Nat's. "You be careful," he told Nat. "I hear Barley Cobb is not going to rest until you're sold into the Deep South. Be *real* careful!"

"Thanks," Nat replied, wishing Delia had told him more. He added to himself, *I hope I'm careful enough*.

EYEWITNESS TO BATTLE

For the next five days, Emily's troubled thoughts never left her. She was now satisfied that Mrs. Yates and Mrs. Wheeler were partly right: She should someday be a teacher. What disturbed her was an ongoing feeling that she should reconsider her decision to never teach in the South.

Brother Appleby said that God had a plan for every life, but everyone had a right to choose whether to accept that plan or not. This thought, and the ongoing tension with Prudence, made Emily keenly aware that things had changed. Strangely, even Hickory Grove didn't really seem like home anymore.

With Christmas less than twelve days away, Emily joined Jessie and her mother in sewing little gifts to be exchanged. Emily thought about that on Friday night as she joined Jessie and her mother in sewing by two coal-oil lamps. Emily was glad that Prudence and Brice had gone to a friend's house for a party. Emily disliked the air of tension that existed whenever Pru was around.

Mrs. Barlow stopped sewing and lowered her voice. "I've been debating whether to tell you girls or not, and I've come to a decision." As Emily and Jessie glanced at her, she continued softly, "Brice must return to his cavalry unit right after Christmas."

Jessie gasped. "You mean go back to the war?"

"Yes," her mother replied. "He got his orders this morning but didn't want to spoil Christmas for the rest of you, so he only told me. But I think you should know."

Emily licked her lips, remembering how many times he had been wounded.

★ ★

Jessie exclaimed, "Oh, I prayed he wouldn't have to go back! I'm afraid for him! Terribly afraid!"

"So am I," Mrs. Barlow replied soberly. "He told me that he had a feeling he might not survive another wound, and he wanted me to know he was ready to meet God."

Emily felt her insides lurch. "Does Prudence know?"

"Oh no," Mrs. Barlow said. "Brice made me promise not to tell her. I know she would like to marry him before he goes back, but he isn't in love with her."

Jessie challenged, "What makes you so sure?"

Her mother hesitated, her eyes flickering to Emily. "A mother sees things others don't. Brice is fond of Pru as a friend but—" She broke off at a knock on the front door.

Jessie asked, "Who could that be?"

"I'll find out," Emily volunteered and took one of the lamps and hurried down the hall, sorry that the conversation had been interrupted. She held the lamp high in one hand and opened the door with the other. A man who looked to be in his fifties asked, "Does Miss Emily Lodge live here?"

"I'm Emily Lodge."

"Two letters for you. One from Virginia."

Emily thanked him, realizing that he was a private letter carrier. Such men had replaced regular service after it was suspended between North and South.

As he said good-night and hurried away, she held the lamp close to the envelopes. One was from Gideon, the other from Mrs. Wheeler.

Emily placed the lamp on a small hall table and opened Mrs. Wheeler's letter first. *My sister insists that I invite you to come visit us. She says if you're as wonderful as I say you are, you should stay with us and go to school here in Chicago. . . .*

That didn't interest Emily, so she stopped reading it and opened Gideon's letter with eager fingers. It was dated three weeks before. *Dear Emily, Hope this reaches you in time for your birthday. Wish I could be there to celebrate with you.* Her eyes darted ahead. *I'm still making trips between Richmond and Fredericksburg. A big battle seems to be shaping up there. . . .*

★ ★

For some reason Emily couldn't explain, she had a sudden feeling of dread. She vainly tried to shake the feeling as she finished the letter.

★　★　★　★　★

The next morning, as fog rose around Fredericksburg, Gideon had picked up Herb Hunter's story from Hugh Dunkerton. Gideon and Zeb had planned to leave right away so the story could be at the *Sun* in time for the afternoon edition. Instead, the boys watched the Confederates scurrying into position on Marye's Heights, a ridge above the town. General Ambrose Burnside's Union troops had crossed the Rappahannock River on pontoon bridges and seized Fredericksburg.

Zeb, in civilian clothes, studied the activities with an experienced eye. He told Gideon, "It's about to start."

Hunter's story confirmed that. Gideon's earlier quick reading of the piece showed that Fredericksburg could be the opening battle in the Union's renewed struggle to seize the capitol at Richmond.

Under General George McClellan, they had earlier failed by advancing up the peninsula to take Richmond from the south. After Lincoln replaced McClellan with Ambrose, the strategy was obviously to strike from the north down to Richmond. It was assumed that when the Confederates lost their capital, the war would be over for the South.

Battle-hardened Zeb watched the preparations with quiet confidence. Gideon's common sense warned him that they should get as far away as possible before the first shot was fired. Still, boyish curiosity and a writer's instinct to see a story happening before his eyes held him fast.

Suddenly Zeb pointed. "Look! Yankees are sending up a war balloon!"

Gideon tensed, recalling his and Zeb's frightening experience of rising into the air, where Union muskets and cannon fired on them. The Union balloonist in foul-weather gear rose higher, his field glasses already sweeping the heights in an effort to find a weakness in the Confederate defenses.

★　★

Zeb turned to a nearby soldier and pointed to his weapon. "Is that a Mississippi rifle?"

The bearded, long-haired veteran corporal replied confidently, "Fifty-four caliber." He aimed at the balloonist.

Gideon remembered his own helpless feeling when Federals had fired on him and Zeb. Fearful that he was about to see an unarmed man killed, Gideon turned away. He heard the shot and shuddered.

"Missed!" Zeb announced.

Relieved, Gideon whirled around and saw the soldier lower his weapon to reload as other small arms began firing. Gideon shifted his eyes to the balloon. He could see the lone passenger crouching down in the basket while the ground crew frantically pulled on the ropes, trying to get him down before a musket ball found its mark.

"I can't watch!" Gideon whispered hoarsely to Zeb. "Let's get out of here!"

An officer yelled, "Hey, you boys! What're you doing here? Get away before you get killed!"

Gideon needed no urging. He turned and ran, glad to hear Zeb right behind him. They had only gone a few feet when the deafening roar of heavy cannon signaled that the battle for Fredericksburg had begun.

★ ★ ★ ★ ★

Nat left John Fletcher in the field and walked around the far side of the Tugwells' house toward the back door. Nat was almost to the steps when suddenly the two family hounds burst from under the back porch, turned right, and charged him.

"Rock! Red! No!" he cried, stopping dead still while fear prickled his skin. He realized that he had approached so quietly they hadn't heard him. They recognized his voice and smell and instantly broke off their rush and loud bawling, but Nat's flesh still seemed alive with goose bumps.

Mrs. Tugwell opened the back door and called, "Are you all right, Nat?"

He swallowed hard before he could answer. "I'm fine, thanks. I've never approached from that direction. I should have known better than to come up so quietly. Ever since Cobb's hounds almost caught me in the swamp, I've had a big fear of dogs."

Ashamed of having confessed this, he added quickly, "Mr. Fletcher sent me to say that he'll be ready in an hour if you want to drive into the village for supplies."

"Thank you, Nat. Oh, before you go back to work, would you mind carrying the slop bucket to the hog?"

"Be glad to." Nat stamped the snow off his shoes and followed her into the kitchen.

She asked, "Will you go to the village with us today and church tomorrow?"

Nat didn't want to risk being alone on the farm where Cobb might catch him. Nat picked up the bucket of milk mixed with table scraps. "Yes, I'd like to do both."

"Good. I've been wanting to talk to you, and we'll have some time on the ride. I wrote Gideon telling him that you could only stay until after Christmas, but I'm hoping your situation has changed and you can stay longer. Any chance of that?"

Nat sadly shook his head. "I know how much he wants to stay in Richmond and learn to be a writer. It's been his ambition since I've known him. If I could, I'd just stay here and help so he could remain in Richmond. But I just can't. You see, I have—"

Mrs. Tugwell interrupted. "You don't have to tell me why." She sighed softly before continuing. "I appreciate how you've helped us so far. But Clara Yates told me at church about the great response you had to your talk to the women's group. She thinks you should become a lawyer and even run for public office if the South loses the war, which she's convinced it will."

"I'm thinking about that," Nat admitted. "But first, I want to repay what the Yateses spent to buy my freedom. Then I want to try finding my brothers."

Mrs. Tugwell sighed. "I understand your dreams, Nat. Well, we'll finish talking on our ride into the village."

Nat nodded and carried the bucket toward the pigpen. He scanned the surrounding countryside, recalling Caesar's warning about Barley Cobb. Somewhere out there, Nat was sure, the slave catcher was watching and waiting.

★ ★

★ ★ ★ ★ ★

In spite of the beautiful December morning, a sense of foreboding haunted Emily from the time she arose. She told herself that she was concerned about Gideon, but it was more than that.

She glanced out her bedchamber window. During the night, a pristine white mantle of new snow had covered the outbuildings and open fields. A glistening series of three-foot-long icicles decorated the eves. Emily had always loved such beauty, but now she barely noticed.

Emily washed her face in the ceramic basin on the nightstand, then went downstairs. She didn't feel any better when she saw Prudence sitting alone at the kitchen table sipping buttermilk.

Emily managed a smile and said, "Good morning. Where is everyone?"

Pru regarded her with thinly veiled dislike and bluntly asked, "When are you moving out?"

Emily was aware that Pru already knew the answer to that, but she reached up into the open cupboard for a glass before replying, "Right after Christmas."

"Why don't you go back to where you came from?"

The words were so unexpected that Emily turned to stare in disbelief. "What?"

"You heard me!" Pru glanced around, but nobody else was near. "Don't you know you don't belong here anymore?"

Emily was surprised at the rudeness, but a disarming reply leaped to her lips. "Prudence, I think you're the prettiest girl I've ever known. You have every feature a girl could ask for, so why do you resent me so much?"

Pru's eyebrows arched as if in astonishment, but that was quickly replaced with a frown. "Don't try to pull that kind of flattery stuff on me! It won't work."

"I'm sincere," Emily assured her. "I know how you feel about Brice, but he's like a big brother to me, not a possible beau."

Pru snapped, "That doesn't change the fact that he said he's going to marry you when you grow up!"

"He was joking!" Emily cried. "Besides, I told you how I feel, so please stop torturing yourself over this!"

"I'm not torturing myself!"

"Sorry, I used a wrong word," Emily hastily replied. "Now, if you'll excuse me, I've got things to do."

She hurriedly replaced the glass and almost ran from the room. *This isn't what I wanted when I came home!* she told herself. *In fact, this isn't home anymore!*

★ ★ ★ ★ ★

On Marye's Heights that morning, the incessant roar of cannon, the thump of exploding shells scattering canister and shrapnel, and the heavy smoke of battle prevented Gideon and Zeb from heading south to Richmond. An officer ordered the boys to get back and take shelter, so they retreated to a safe distance as the fog lifted and the fight intensified.

Zeb shouted above the rattle of musketry and the boom of cannon, "Look at those stupid Yankees! They're getting ready to get themselves killed by the thousands!"

Gideon didn't want to look, but he realized that this was probably the only chance he would ever have to eyewitness a battle. He told himself that he should watch enough to write a report for the newspaper. This time he would not let Max steal it from him. So Gideon cautiously raised his head above the log where he and Zeb had found shelter.

"We couldn't ask for a better place to see," Zeb said matter-of-factly. "That's General Lee's headquarters on the right. Marye's house is that big two-story place down below. In the distance, you can see the houses of Fredericksburg and the Rappahannock River. But look back closer this way, just past Marye's house. See them?"

Zeb had recovered from his emotional battle scars, but he became highly distressed at seeing what was about to happen. He exclaimed, "I'm glad I'm not a bluecoat soldier down there! The officers are getting ready to send them charging against our lines, but the Yankees don't have a chance!"

Gideon didn't reply. He tried to control his emotions rising from the horrible realization that thousands of men were about to die before his eyes.

★ ★

Pointing, Zeb continued, "See that sunken road there by that stone wall? Our boys are protected by both that road and the wall. We've also got the high ground, with cannon from the heights to pour down on them. It's plain suicide to—"

He broke off as the first wave of Union troops began charging toward the sunken road and the stone wall. It seemed unreal to Gideon. Young men ran yelling, armed only with rifles, to attack well-protected Confederate positions.

The entire line of defenders began firing. Smoke from their muskets puffed up above their heads split seconds before minié balls mowed men down like summer wheat falling before the sickle. The smoke expanded, making them hard to see. But the unprotected Federals were clearly visible. One moment they were yelling, brave soldiers clinging together; the next second, many were hit. They staggered and collapsed, sprawled grotesquely on the ground as their blood sank into the soil.

While some fell, never to rise again, the screams of the wounded mingled with the sounds of small arms and the heavy roaring of cannon, which further devastated the Union lines.

Zeb cried, "Look at them—still coming! Wave after wave, but they don't stand a chance. Why do their officers keep sending troops to die so needlessly?"

The scene didn't seem real to Gideon. It was hard to make himself believe that he was really watching human beings horribly reduced to twisted and torn lumps as they crumpled across their fallen comrades.

Suddenly, the reality of the horrific sight finally hit Gideon so hard that his stomach rebelled. He turned away, crawling on hands and knees a few feet before violent sickness overcame him.

★　★　★　★　★

Later that night, Gideon was so emotionally drained that he could barely stand. Forever engraved in his memory were images of twelve thousand Yankees falling in a vain attempt to breach Confederate lines. The Confederate casualties were less than half that, giving them a great but extremely bloody victory.

Gideon and Zeb made their way to the Dunkerton farmhouse,

where they planned to spend the night and possibly get another story from Herb Hunter.

Zeb spoke soberly. "This is the first fight I ever saw where I wasn't likely to be killed. And you can write a great story for your paper from what you saw."

"No," Gideon said, still in shock. "I stayed to watch so I could do just that, but now I realize I can't! I could never write about what I saw today! I never even want to think about it again, ever!"

★　★　★　★　★

The boys got slightly lost and were late in reaching the farmhouse. Herb Hunter was there ahead of them in a dirty uniform. His face was drawn and pale, almost gray. His left pants leg was bloody from a hole in it.

"What happened?" Gideon cried upon seeing Hunter's bloody uniform and pain-filled face.

"Took a Yankee minié ball in my leg," the correspondent replied weakly. "The surgeon said I'm losing a lot of blood, but I told him I had to do something before he could treat me."

Gideon warned, "It's still bleeding! I think—"

"I know," Hunter interrupted. "I'll have it treated now, but first I had to get the battle story to you." He held up a stack of papers and added with a sigh, "You've got to get to Richmond first because . . . Well, this may be the last story I ever write."

TERROR IN THE SWAMP

As daybreak touched the eastern horizon, Gideon noticed it had rained hard in the night. He and Zeb climbed into a wagon driven by one of Hugh Dunkerton's slaves. As the mule plodded along the muddy road, both boys were quiet, each recalling the dramatic events of the day before. Gideon was especially distressed over what had happened to Hunter.

Zeb finally asked, "You going to be all right?"

"I hope so," Gideon replied miserably. "I didn't sleep much last night. I kept seeing those waves of Yankees being shot down as they charged our lines. It was so horrible! Then Mr. Hunter—"

Zeb interrupted, "Now you know how I felt when you found me in the hospital. I can't tell you how many men got killed all around me before I got hit myself."

Gideon laid a hand on his friend's shoulder. "I'm glad you're all right now."

"Thanks." Zeb paused, then added, "I'm real sorry about Mr. Hunter. He might have lived if he had first gone to the surgeons instead of writing his story."

Gideon vainly tried to block out the memory of the correspondent's blood seeping into his boot. Sighing, Gideon said, "I would never have had a chance to learn anything about writing for a newspaper if he hadn't helped. I owe him a lot."

Reaching inside his coat pocket, Gideon took out the sheets of paper where Hunter had written his final story. "Well," Gideon continued, "at least we'll get this to the *Sun* for him. But I have to go home without a single published story that the editor knows is mine."

Zeb declared, "I still think you should tell him about Max stealing your stuff."

"No. It would still be my word against his, and besides, I don't want to . . . Listen!"

"Cannon!" Zeb exclaimed, instinctively ducking and glancing upward. "Firing right over our heads!"

"But why?" Gideon asked, his voice rising in alarm. "The battle's over!"

"Maybe Yankees covering their retreat." Zeb twisted in the wagon bed. "Driver . . ."

Gideon didn't hear the rest. A bright flash and a violent explosion to the side of the road hurled the wagon into the air, instantly ejecting the passengers.

Gideon instinctively released Hunter's papers and thrust his hands out to break his fall. Pages fluttered around him like startled pigeons. When he hit the soft, muddy ground, his arms crumpled and he landed face down. He lay there momentarily stunned and tasting mud.

As his head slowly cleared, he realized Zeb was kneeling beside him, pleading, "Gid! Are you all right?"

Gideon wiped his mouth with muddy hands. "Yes. You?"

"I landed in some bushes; just got a few scratches."

Gideon sat up. The dawn light showed the wagon upside down and badly splintered. The mule stood nearby, apparently unhurt. Gideon asked, "What about the driver?"

"Ran off." Zeb pointed back the way they had come. "I guess he was more scared than we were. Can you stand?"

"I think so." Gideon slowly rose to his feet and grinned at his friend. "We'd . . . oh! Mr. Hunter's story!" Gideon scanned the area and groaned. He retrieved two pages that had landed in a mud puddle. The ink had run and the pages were streaked with mud. Frantically, Gideon found other pages that were soggy and unreadable.

Gideon mournfully checked the salvaged sheets and groaned in deep distress. "Hunter gave his life for this story, and it's ruined!

★ ★

Every page is smeared! I can't even make out a single word!"

Zeb asked, "Didn't you read that story last night?"

"Yes, but I can't remember all of it."

"Of course not, but you can remember some of it and add some of what you saw yesterday."

"Me?" Gideon cried. "I can't do that! I'll just have to tell the editor what happened. . . ."

"No!" Zeb's tone was firm. "Your friend wanted that story to get in the paper so much that he died for it. It's not your fault that it's gone, but you can rewrite it!"

"Even if I could," Gideon protested, "the editor will recognize that it's not Mr. Hunter's writing style!"

"I didn't mean you should try to fool him," Zeb explained. "But I'm sure the editor will want to know what you and Mr. Hunter saw firsthand. You're a good writer, and I know you can do it."

"I don't know . . ." Gideon said doubtfully.

"Besides," Zeb added, "think of it this way. Maybe Mr. Hunter is still helping you get a little closer to your writing goal."

As Gideon hesitated, Zeb added, "You can start the writing in your head while I unharness the mule. If he will let us ride double and bareback to Richmond, you can write the story in time for tomorrow's deadline. Then we'll find a way to get the mule back to the farmer."

★　★　★　★　★

Fresh snow in the night covered the Illinois prairie on Sunday morning as Emily rode the sleigh to church with the Barlows. The knowledge that Hickory Grove was no longer Emily's home had given her a sleepless night.

If this isn't my home, she wondered, *where is? I don't want to be put in an orphanage!*

The sleigh bells stopped jingling as Brice reined in across the road from Old Bethel. He removed the lap robes from his mother and sister and helped them step down.

"You two go on ahead," he told them. "I want a word with Emily before we go in."

Surprised, Emily glanced around and was glad to see that Prudence hadn't yet arrived.

Brice climbed into the closed sleigh and sat down by Emily. He said, "I don't know how to say this right, so I'll say it straight out. After Christmas, I have to return to duty. I want you to know that I appreciated your praying for me in the past, and I hope you'll continue to do so."

Emily stirred uneasily. "Of course I will."

"Thanks." He hesitated, then dropped his voice. "Emily, I also want you to know that I consider you a very special person."

She thought she knew what he meant but couldn't be sure. She lowered her eyes without replying.

He continued, "I can't say more than that, but I had to say it just in case . . . well, just in case."

"You'll be all right," she replied, not at all sure that she had any reason to say that.

"I hope to be," Brice assured her. "Will you still write me and let me know how you're doing?"

Emily hesitated, feeling a twinge of conscience because of Gideon and Pru. The sound of bells coming down the rural road made Emily glance back. She recognized Pru's cutter. Emily replied hurriedly, "Yes, Brice. Now we'd better go inside."

"Of course." He stepped out and offered his hand.

She took it but quickly released it when her feet crunched onto the snow. Prudence was close enough now that Emily could see the anger in her face as she turned the horse toward the hitching rail.

Fearful of another unpleasant confrontation with Pru, Emily hurried toward the church, where several people stood outside the front door. Emily didn't look back but heard Pru's shrill voice just as a lone rider on a lathered horse trotted down the road.

"It just came over the wires that there was a real bad battle yesterday at Fredericksburg. The winner isn't known yet."

The rider rode on to spread the word while Emily's heart skipped a couple of beats. *Gideon probably was there! Oh, I hope he's safe!*

★ ★ ★ ★ ★

While John Fletcher finished dressing for church, Nat volunteered to harness the mule to the wagon. Nat saw Hercules well out in the field. Nat started after the animal, watching out for Cobb. There was nothing in the fields except Hercules, and he moved toward the fence with the swamp beyond.

"Whoa, Hercules!" Nat called as the animal passed the small wooded area where Cobb had previously ambushed Nat. The mule displayed the contrary temperament of his kind and ignored the command. Nat followed, circling wide around the grove of trees that now blocked his view of the Tugwell house. He was relieved that there was no sign of man or hounds among the winter-bare trunks. The silent swamp beyond the fence line showed only a vast expanse of tall trees and tangles of dense underbrush.

Nat got within a few feet of Hercules when the mule moved just out of reach, stopped, and looked back at Nat. "Whoa!" he ordered. "Whoa! Stand still!"

Hercules again let Nat get almost within touching distance, then tossed his head and moved off again. Nat followed and extended his hand as if offering grain. "Whoa, I say! You're going to make everyone late for church!"

The mule turned his long ears attentively toward Nat, but again moved out of reach. Nat doggedly followed, trying to keep from losing his patience. "What's got into you, Hercules?" he asked, trying to make the words sound gentle and pleasant. "You're not going to have to pull a plow today, just a wagon."

His words snapped off at the sudden explosive bawling of a hound. Whirling in great alarm, Nat saw Barley Cobb with four hounds leaving the grove of trees. The dogs strained against their collars and the chains that held them back, but Cobb didn't hurry.

He called, "Ye cain't git away this time, black boy! So stop a'fore I sic them dawgs on ye an' they tear ye plumb to pieces!"

Nat's instinct was to run toward the house, but the slave catcher had obviously anticipated that. He laughed and moved to cut off Nat's escape that way. Whirling, he took a few running steps and made a frantic grab for the mule's mane. Nat's fingers touched

★ ★

the long, coarse hair, but Hercules jerked his head away and trotted off.

Nat realized he had only one choice. He ran hard toward the swamp, with the hounds yelping behind him.

★ ★ ★ ★ ★

The church was uncomfortably hot from the woodburning stove and the men, women, and children who had crowded inside for the annual pageant. Brother Appleby's sermon concerned the true meaning of Christmas. Emily was unmoved until he neared his conclusion.

"If you had gone to the Bethlehem manger with the wise men to offer gifts, what would you bring? Why, the very best, most precious thing you have. And what's that? Your life. God gave the greatest gift of all: the Babe in the manger who came with a mission. I believe that each one of us is born with a God-given mission in life."

Emily was emotionally moved as the pastor continued.

"No matter how young you are or how old you are, I can think of nothing greater in this holy season than to discover, and then give your life to fulfilling, the cause for which you are here on earth."

Emily was so engrossed in the personal application that she wasn't even aware that the parishioners around her were standing for the benediction.

Jessie leaned over to whisper, "What's wrong?"

Emily blinked, looked around, and quickly stood. She whispered, "I was just thinking about something."

"Tell me later," Jessie said. "Let's go."

"You go ahead. I'd like to go to my family's graves for a few minutes—alone."

"Don't do that! It'll only make you sadder!"

"I won't be long. I'll meet you at the sleigh."

Emily made her way through the happy crowd, deliberately avoiding making eye contact with Pru or Brice. After a brief stop in the cloakroom, Emily walked across the snow-covered cemetery, her mind filled with troubled thoughts.

★ ★

Light snow was falling as she made her solitary way to her family's graves. She knelt, closed her eyes, and bowed her head in silent prayer.

Lord, all I wanted was to return here to live, but things have changed. It not's really my home anymore. I'm only held here by memories of my family who rest under this stone. I don't understand why they're all dead and I'm still alive. I'd like to know why.

Emily paused expectantly but heard only the rising wind in the trees and felt the gentle kiss of snowflakes on her face. Fragments of thoughts flashed through her mind. *Cleobulus. Teacher. Mrs. Wheeler's letter extending her sister's invitation to come to Chicago . . .*

The sound of footsteps on snow made Emily's eyes pop open. She was startled to see Brice approaching.

He said, "I didn't mean to disturb you, but I had to be sure you're all right."

She rose to her feet. "I'm fine, thanks." She glanced toward the church but didn't see Pru. Turning her gaze back to Brice, she impulsively asked, "Do you think God has a plan for every life?"

He shrugged. "I don't know. Before the war, I thought I had life pretty well figured out. But after seeing so many men die all around me, I'm not so sure anymore. That's even after I've given it lots of thought while I was a Rebel prisoner and wounded in the hospital. I am sure about one thing: I want you to be happy, Emily. I want God's best for you."

"Thanks," she murmured, lowering her eyes, unsure if she should say anything more. When she lifted her gaze again, Brice was striding across the cemetery toward the sleigh. Pru stood there, her face filled with fury.

In that instant, everything clicked into place for Emily. She hesitated only briefly before knowing what she must do. She walked purposefully toward Brice and Pru.

★ ★ ★ ★ ★

Nat's lungs burned from running so hard across the Tugwells' field. In terror, he vaulted over the boundary fence and plunged into the swamp. The cold had partially solidified the deep peat, so his feet didn't sink into the muck as they had when he and the slave girl Sarah had fled from Cobb's hounds. With heart thudding against his ribs, Nat glanced back. Cobb unhurriedly followed, holding back the eager hounds.

Nat understood why. *He wants me to get as far away from the house as possible before he turns the dogs loose! If I live, he'll sell me back into slavery!*

With that realization, Nat slowed to catch his breath, although that was hard because the hounds were bawling loudly, eager to get to him. *There must be a way to save myself,* he thought, *but how?* No ideas came as he struggled through the dense underbrush.

Nat passed a leaning dead tree trunk about twelve feet high. He paused briefly and rested his hand on the snag as he looked back. It creaked ominously and tipped even farther off balance. Nat jerked his hand away, still watching Cobb following confidently. He forcibly held the hounds in check.

Nat started running again. He leaped a downed log and landed on what seemed to be solid ground covered by snow. But it crumpled under his weight and he sank to his knees in an icy quagmire.

He tried to lift one foot, but the effort drove the other deeper into the marsh. Nat heard Cobb let out a triumphant shout that was almost lost in the dogs' eager bawling. Nat grabbed hold of nearby brush and tried to pull himself free but couldn't. He was caught like an animal in a trap.

FROM DESPAIR
TO HOPE

Panting with futile exertion, Nat gave up trying to lift his legs from the icy swamp trap. He switched to grabbing double handfuls of the adjacent brush in hopes of pulling himself free. He ignored his bleeding and torn palms but could not avoid glancing back in terror at Barley Cobb and his excited hounds.

Cobb quickly bent to unsnap the dogs' leashes. But in their wild excitement, they leaped against their leashes and thrashed around in frenzied circles, trying to break free. One hound dashed around the trunk of the twelve-foot leaning tree snag, which had tottered when Nat leaned against it minutes before. This tightened the hound's chain, so he frantically fought against it, pulling away from Cobb, who was fighting to hang on to the other end of the leash.

The snag's rotted root system exploded from the soft earth. Cobb saw the danger and tried to leap out of the way, but the snag twisted in midair. It crashed at an angle, catching Cobb from behind and driving him face first into the spongy mess. He screamed in pain and terror as the log settled on his lower back, but as an experienced hunter, he instinctively held on to the dogs' chains.

Good! Nat thought. *If he doesn't let go of those hounds . . .* Nat didn't finish his thought, knowing what the dogs would do to him if they caught him as he was. Nat rapidly extended his lower hand above the other to get another grip higher on the brush. He felt his trapped feet slowly inch upward in the muck.

It's working! The joyful thought spurred him to again reach higher on the brush and pull harder. *A little bit more . . . There!*

★　★

165

Nat's feet came free with a sucking sound. He slid from the trap onto the clump of brush. Panting hard, he leaped to his feet, relieved to feel that he was on semisolid ground. He started to run again but looked back to where the hounds wildly leaped against their chains that Cobb still held.

Nat's gaze shifted to the heavy snag pinning the slave catcher to the earth. He raised an imploring hand.

"He'p me!" he howled. "Ye cain't let me die!"

Nat was suspicious that it might be a trick to get him to come closer. But another glance at the snag showed Cobb was unable to free himself from the crushing weight.

Nat hesitated, recalling when Cobb and his hounds had chased him and Sarah through this same swamp. Nat bitterly remembered the other times Cobb had pursued or terrorized him.

He brought this on himself! Nat thought. *He deserves it! Besides, now's my chance to get away. But if he turns those dogs loose* . . . Nat refused to finish the thought, abruptly torn between two very hard choices.

★　★　★　★　★

Emily approached the sleigh, where Brice and Prudence stood facing each other, unaware of Emily's approach in the lightly falling snow. She heard Pru's shrill voice.

"Nothing has been right," she cried to Brice. "Not since she came here! She's a child, yet she's ruining my life—and ours!"

Emily slowed, aware that the couple hadn't yet noticed her approach.

Brice said firmly, "I'm sorry you're upset, Pru, but you're wrong! Emily is not ruining your life. It's your attitude that's hurting our relationship!"

"So now it's my fault!" Pru shrilled.

Patiently, Brice replied, "I didn't say that! And stop trying to make an issue out of this!"

"You can't talk to me that way!" Pru snapped. "I want her to go away so we can be like we were before—" She interrupted herself upon catching sight of Emily.

Pru cried, "Why did you come back here? You're not welcome! Don't you know that, Emily?"

"Prudence!" Brice exclaimed. "That's not true, so watch your tongue!"

Emily walked up to face her and spoke quietly. "Ever since I left here to live with my relatives in Virginia, I have longed with all my heart to come back here to my home. But it's not my home anymore, so, Pru, you're going to get your wish. I'm going away!"

"No, Emily!" Brice exclaimed. "This is your home! Nobody has the right to drive you away!"

Emily shook her head, causing snowflakes to fly from her bonnet. "I'm not being driven away. I'm going because I'm no longer needed here, but I know where I will be needed."

"Please don't leave!" Brice pleaded.

Prudence had remained quiet since her last outburst, but Emily could see mixed reaction in the other girl's eyes. They softened toward Emily but flared up at Brice. "You're making a fool of yourself!"

"Stop it, both of you!" Emily ordered firmly. "Now, if you'll both just listen without interrupting, I'll try to explain how I came to this decision."

★ ★ ★ ★ ★

For several seconds, Nat grappled with his primal urge to escape versus the slave catcher's dangerous plight. The hounds repeatedly leaped against their chains, trying to reach Nat.

He watched Cobb vainly push against the log with one hand and hang on to the frantic dogs' leashes with the other. "Please!" he begged. "Ye got to he'p me real quick-like! I'm plumb busted up inside!"

Nat's feelings erupted in a blunt, heartfelt question. "Why should I?" But the moment he said it, he remembered Brother Tynes' sermon on doing to others what you would have them do to you.

Cobb screeched, "I'm bein' plumb good to ye 'cause I could jist let them dawgs go and they'd tear ye to ribbins! But I ain't done that 'cause if'n ye don't he'p me, I'll die."

★ ★

Nat knew that the slave catcher was right on both points, but the animosity between them was so great that Nat hesitated.

Cobb again vainly pushed against the log, then turned, panting, toward Nat. "I reckon ye ain't got no good reason fer to he'p me after what I done to ye," Cobb admitted, "but ye cain't jest leave me here to die. If'n ye he'p me, I kin give me bonded word that I won't never chase ner bother ye ag'in!"

Nat had already made an instant decision to help, but not for Cobb's offer. Rather, Nat was motivated by what he had heard at the church service. Now he would show his faith by his actions.

He said, "Tie the dogs so they can't get to me, then I'll try to move that log."

"Hurry! Hurry!" Cobb screeched, his face contorting in pain as he struggled to transfer his end of the leashes from his hand to a stub of limb on the log.

"Thar!" Cobb panted, turning from the dogs and trying to twist sideways to push with both hands against the log pinning him down. "That oughta hold 'em. Now, git me outa here a'fore I up and die!"

Nat rubbed his bleeding and muddy hands along his sleeves as if he could rub off the gooseflesh. Then, with the hounds eagerly leaping against their chains to reach him, Nat cautiously approached the far end of the snag. His eyes never left the dogs.

★　★　★　★　★

The snow fell harder, but Emily didn't notice as she began explaining to Brice and Pru, "In all my dreams, I never expected to leave here after I got back from the Confederacy. But almost from the moment I arrived here, I saw many changes. Like the house where I grew up, now falling down—taking everything except my memories.

"At my family's graves, I asked God what I had so often asked before. Why are they all gone and I alone am still alive? Well, I still don't know why they're dead, but just moments ago, praying over in the snow, I sensed what I must do with my life—at least the next step."

Emily hurried on, hoping not to be interrupted until she had finished pouring out the words that had suddenly filled her so full that they tumbled over each other.

She summarized her tutoring experiences in Virginia.

Emily concluded, "Since coming back to Hickory Grove, I've learned that there are some places where you can't ever really return. There comes a time to move on, to let go of the past and take hold of the future. For me, that means becoming a teacher."

"A schoolteacher?" Brice asked.

"Yes, but not here," Emily replied. "You see, if the South loses the war, which seems likely, and all slaves will be freed by President Lincoln, then those black children will need to be educated along with white ones."

"Black children?" Pru questioned. "Where are you going to find any around here?"

"I'm not," Emily said. "That's what I was leading up to say. I'll teach in the South."

"No!" Brice exclaimed. "I've seen so much of the Confederacy already torn up by the war! By the time it's over, the whole South could be in total ruins!"

"Yes, it could," Emily admitted. "But people will still live there. They'll rebuild and have children who must learn how to read and write. They'll need educating, since that holds their future. So I'm going to Chicago to learn to be a teacher, then I'll go back to the South."

"No!" Brice cried. "You don't have to go!"

"Yes, I do, right after Christmas," Emily answered calmly. "It's no longer against my will. I want to do it. Brice, you will always be in my prayers. And, Pru, I would like us to be friends, so I won't stand between your friendship with Brice. I—"

"Pardon me!" Brice interrupted crisply. "But I have something to say about who my friends are!"

"Of course!" Emily hurriedly replied. "I just meant that I want to be friends with everyone; especially you two. I will, if you'll both let me. What do you say?"

The snowflakes silently fell on the three of them while Emily waited for their response.

★ ★

Brice spoke first. "I say, let's all be friends." He turned questioning eyes to Pru.

She nodded and smiled. "Friends," she declared. "We'll all be friends."

★　★　★　★　★

The swamp echoed with hounds' bawling as they leaped against their leashes to get at Nat while he mightily tried to lift the tree snag from the slave catcher.

"Yore a-killin' me!" Cobb screeched. "Ever' time ye lift back thar, ye put all the weight on me!"

"Sorry, but I'm doing the best I can!" Nat protested, easing the end of the log down again and looking around for something that might work. "I think I see something that should help."

Nat had to walk within three feet of the nearest dog, which absolutely sent it into gyrations as it lunged against the leash, snapping at Nat. Carefully, his eyes on the hound, Nat grabbed one end of a stout limb.

Grasping it firmly, he quickly backed up and tested the limb's sturdiness by pressing down hard on it. "I think this will do," he told Cobb and slid the narrow end across a small dead log to serve as a prop.

Still leery of the dogs, Nat had to turn his back on them while they raged less than three feet away. He told Cobb in a trembling voice, "When I pry down on this end, and you feel the weight lift, drag yourself out from under there as fast as you can. Understand?"

"Yes! Yes! Jis' git me outa this!" Cobb replied and immediately began cursing.

That aggravated Nat, but he carefully placed both hands on his end of the limb and prepared to throw his weight down on it. "Ready?" he shouted. "Now!"

The far end of the pry log sank into the soft peat, but Nat kept shoving down with all his strength. "It's moving!" he cried. "It's lifting! Get ready! Now crawl!"

Using his elbows to drag his upper body, Cobb wiggled free, then cried, "I cain't move my legs!"

★　★

Nat didn't realize he was perspiring until a salty drop trickled into his right eye, making it burn. "Keep trying!" Nat instructed, again fighting an urge to run because he had done enough.

Slowly, grimacing with pain, the slave catcher got his legs moving. He carefully stood and felt his back and ribs. "Reckon I ain't as bad off as I done thought," he admitted. "The ground done give way under me some."

Nat said, "I'll go get the mule and sled to take you out of here." He turned toward the Tugwells' home, but Cobb's voice stopped him.

"Boy, why ain't ye a-runnin' away whilst ye kin?"

"I don't know," Nat honestly admitted. "I guess I just couldn't leave you here, because if it had been me under that log, I'd want you to do the same."

Cobb's eyes suddenly glittered and a sneer touched his bearded face. "Nah, boy, that ain't it. Ye done it 'cause yer kind is jest plain stupid. Ye cain't do nothin' 'cause they ain't a brain in yer head."

Nat stared in disbelief as Cobb turned away toward the dogs still leaping against their chains. He said over his shoulder, "Muh dawgs need a few bites o' black hide fer runnin' ye down. Reckon they kin learn ye somethin' a'fore I sell what's left o' ye!"

As Cobb bent over the first dog to unsnap his chain, Nat spun around in terror and started to run. But he knew it was impossible to escape the animals. He had taken only a couple of steps when he heard the click of a pistol being cocked, but he didn't remember Cobb having a weapon.

A voice commanded, "Cobb! Stop! Don't move!"

Nat swiveled his head to see John Fletcher step out from behind the trunk of a maple tree. Cobb froze, his hand on the dog's leash.

"Thank God!" Nat exclaimed. Fletcher approached with a pistol in his remaining hand.

"Cobb, step away from the dog!" Fletcher ordered. As the slave catcher obeyed, Fletcher said grimly, "I heard and saw enough to put you in jail or at least run you out of the country!"

"Ah, ye know I was jist a-funnin' the boy," he protested in a whining tone. "I weren't really gonna turn them dawgs loose on him."

Fletcher didn't reply, but without taking his eyes off the captive, he said, "Nat, I'm proud of you for what you just did."

Nat's pulse was still racing when he answered rather ruefully, "You wouldn't have said that if you could have known my thoughts just before I remembered something I heard an old exhorter say."

Fletcher nodded but spoke to Cobb. "You hang on tight to those dogs while Nat and I walk you back to the house. If one of them so much as snaps at—"

"They won't git away!" Cobb broke in. "I give ye muh bonded word—"

Fletcher's laugh cut him off. "Nat and I know about your word, Cobb. But ours is different. Trust me on that. Now, get a good grip on those chains and start walking!"

As Cobb obeyed, Fletcher said, "Nat, I think things are going to be a lot better for you from now on."

Nat's face split in a wide grin. "I believe you're right! Things are going to be a whole lot better!"

★ ★ ★ ★ ★

The next morning, Gideon arrived at the *Sun* with a sheaf of papers in his hand. His mindset had changed so much that he was almost glad to see Max Hassler sitting at the front desk.

"Max," Gideon said quietly, showing the papers, "I've got a story for the editor. I'll take it in."

"Now, just a minute!" Max replied, jumping to his feet as Gideon started past the desk. "You can't—"

"Can't what?" Gideon demanded in a low, hard tone.

Max drew back slightly. "I'll take it in for you."

"No, thanks. I have to explain something—"

The inner door opened, interrupting him. The editor said to Max, "Run down to the . . ." Buford Kerr left his thought unfinished. Instead, he turned to Gideon and asked, "You look terrible! What happened?"

Gideon replied simply, "Mr. Hunter is dead."

"Dead?" Kerr exclaimed. "When? How?"

Gideon briefly explained, adding, "But before he died, he wrote a story about the battle."

"Is that it?" Kerr asked, taking the papers from Gideon's hands.

"No, sir. I was going to say that he gave his pages to me, but there was an accident. They were destroyed. But I was also at the battle, and so I wrote—"

"Shut up and let me read this!" Kerr ordered, his eyes expertly skimming the pages. Slowly, his brow wrinkled and a frown crept across his face. He looked up at Gideon. "You wrote this?"

"Yes, sir. Took me most of yesterday and last night, but—"

"You have a unique style, Tugwell," Kerr broke in. "Clear and tight but with feeling. Just like . . ." he shifted his gaze to Max, "just like a couple of stories you wrote, Max; one about a wounded drummer boy, and another about a girl who works in the munitions factory."

Gideon watched Max swallow hard before saying, "Thank you, Mr. Kerr. I worked hard—"

"You're a liar!" Kerr's explosive words made both boys jump. "You think I'm a fool, Max? Writers have styles that are as unique as faces. I hate liars! Take your things and get out of here right now!"

"But, Mr. Kerr!"

"Out, Max! Now!" the editor yelled, pointing toward the front door.

Gideon stepped aside as the other boy hurried out, his head down and shoulders slumped.

Kerr's tone softened. "Tugwell, I wondered why you showed so much interest in writing when you first came, yet you never turned in a single story, not even after I offered to pay you stringer rates. Come on into my office. You have some stringing money coming."

Kerr led the way, saying over his shoulder, "I now have an opening for a promising boy who wants to learn how to be a writer. You want the job?"

Gideon almost shouted, "Oh yes, sir! I—" His words snapped off as he remembered. He added sadly, "I'm sorry. I can't. My family needs me to help on the farm."

★ ★

The editor carefully placed Gideon's pages on the desk before sitting down at it. He motioned for Gideon to sit. For the first time Gideon could remember, Kerr spoke softly. "Tell me about it in thirty seconds, and don't leave anything out."

Gideon wasn't sure Mr. Kerr was joking, but he didn't take any chances. Gideon quickly summarized his family's situation. When he finished, he sighed heavily.

Kerr absently tugged at his beard. "I understand, Gideon. Family first." Reaching into his desk, the editor opened the drawstring on a small leather pouch that clinked. "Here's a double eagle. I hope twenty dollars will pay for your stories that Max stole."

"Thanks," Gideon said, accepting the coin. "This will repay what my mother loaned me to come here."

Kerr held up another smaller one. "Here's a half eagle for your integrity. I sometimes pay for intrinsic values as well as tangible work performed."

Gideon murmured his thanks, thinking that now he could not only repay his mother, he would also have enough left over for some Christmas presents. But his heart was leaving behind one of the best opportunities of his life.

Kerr got to his feet. "I tell you what, Gideon. If you'll write some stories from your hometown area, I'll try to use them and pay stringer rates. The first one I'd like is various people's reactions to what they think will happen when President Lincoln's Emancipation Proclamation becomes effective New Year's Day. Do a survey of slave owners, freedmen, and even slaves, if you can get them to talk to you. You want to do that?"

Gideon had stood up right after the editor did. "Yes, sir! Very much!"

"Good!" Kerr lightly tapped the pages on his desk. "Now I'm going to do something unusual and not only run your story about Fredericksburg, but I'll add a sidebar telling about you and why you wrote it. That will honor Herb Hunter's valiant last act as a newspaper correspondent, and you'll be able to take a copy of this story home with you. This will prove that you're on your way to becoming a writer. Is that all right with you?"

Gideon couldn't answer because his emotions suddenly threatened to get away from him. He was so overwhelmed that he could only nod.

"One last thing, Gideon," the editor said. "If you can somehow work things out at home so they won't need you beyond Christmas, I'll hold this job open. If you're back here by the day after New Year's, the job is yours."

Totally overwhelmed, Gideon was still speechless, and he thrust out his right hand and nodded vigorously as the editor shook it. Gideon abruptly turned and hurried out before his heart exploded from pure joy.

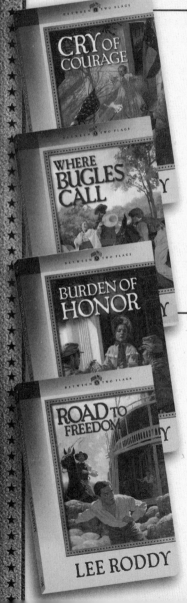